A
Harlequin
Romance

OTHER
Harlequin Romances

by MARGARET MAYO

1980—DESTINY PARADISE

Many of these titles are available at your local bookseller,
or through the Harlequin Reader Service.

For a free catalogue listing all available Harlequin Romances,
send your name and address to:

HARLEQUIN READER SERVICE,
M.P.O. Box 707, Niagara Falls, N.Y. 14302
Canadian address: Stratford, Ontario, Canada N5A 6W4

or use order coupon at back of books.

SHADES OF AUTUMN

by

MARGARET MAYO

Harlequin Books

TORONTO • LONDON • NEW YORK • AMSTERDAM • SYDNEY • WINNIPEG

Original hardcover edition published in 1976
by Mills & Boon Limited

ISBN 0-373-01996-3

Harlequin edition published August, 1976

Printed in U.S.A.

CHAPTER ONE

LAURA was the only passenger to alight and with the departure of the train she felt suddenly alone and more than a little apprehensive. The whole place appeared deserted. Why was there no one to meet her? Hadn't Brad Stuart received her letter?

She walked slowly towards a grey stone building at the other end of the platform. Presumably the station office, although with its neatly dug flower beds and curtained windows, it looked more like a country cottage.

As she approached, a bent old man in the navy uniform of British Rail appeared. He looked at Laura curiously before taking her ticket. 'Visiting relatives?'

Laura shook her head, looking over his shoulder along the road leading from the station. 'I hoped there would be someone to meet me. Someone from Leastone Hall. Is it far?'

'About two miles. See yonder hills?' A gnarled finger pointed in the distance. 'Mr. Stuart's house lies over there. It's a fair walk, but you won't miss it. A big black and white place—are you a friend of the family?'

'No. I'm Mr. Stuart's new secretary. Isn't there a bus?' Laura felt dismayed at the prospect of a two-mile walk. She wasn't exactly dressed for the occasion.

' 'Fraid not—no buses on a Sunday.'

'A taxi, then?' Surely she could get some sort of transport?

'Not today.' He looked doubtfully at her high-heeled shoes and the suitcase at her side. 'You could phone

5

Mr. Stuart, ask him to send someone. He probably forgot about the buses.'

'No—I'll walk.' Anger against her future employer rose quickly. If Brad Stuart hadn't thought to arrange transport she wouldn't lower herself by asking. He must have known the difficulties she would encounter.

Head held high, she marched out of the station, noticing briefly the village to her left. Timbered cottages, the church spire thrusting upwards and the people making their way home after morning service. At any other time she would have been entranced, but at the moment she was too annoyed to give it more than a cursory glance.

Again Laura wondered whether she had done the right thing in moving out of her London flat. It had seemed a good idea at the time and the salary Brad Stuart offered was staggeringly high, which had certainly helped her decide. But still persisting at the back of her mind, like a warning bell, were David's words that Brad Stuart had difficulty in keeping a secretary. There must be a reason, and she wished now that she had taken the trouble to find out why.

If only David had not decided to emigrate there would have been no need for her to change her job. For three years, ever since leaving secretarial college at the age of eighteen, she had been his secretary. He worked as a freelance advertising consultant and she loved the variety of work involved. She was shocked when suddenly he told her that he was closing down the business, as she was a little in love with David herself. Unfortunately for her he was happily married, so she had been forced to keep her feelings hidden.

It was David who suggested she might like to work for his friend who lived in Shropshire and impulsively

6

she had agreed. She had never really settled in London and the thought of living in the country again was tempting.

Now she began to regret her decision. The road which had looked deceptively level when she started was gradually climbing and her legs ached with the un-accustomed exercise.

'I've half a mind to return to London,' she said aloud. 'If this is the way he treated his other secretaries it's no wonder they didn't stay. What does he think we are? Amazons?' She flung herself down on the grass verge with scant regard for the new green suit in which she had dressed so carefully a few hours earlier. Kicking off her shoes, she ruefully examined her blistered heels. 'How shall I finish the journey?' she asked herself in dismay.

The road was deserted. Sadly she realised that no traffic had passed her at all during the time she had been walking. Brad Stuart certainly lived far from civilisation. David had not prepared her for that.

Painfully continuing her journey, Laura wished she had never agreed to come in the first place. The road now rose steeply as it formed a pass between the hills. Almost on the verge of collapse, she rounded a bend, breathing a sigh of relief as she glimpsed the house between the trees.

Pushing open the heavy iron gates, Laura limped along the drive, its edges encroached on either side by glossy rhododendron bushes and heavy woodland, temporarily blocking the black and white building from view.

Laura stopped, changing her suitcase to her other hand. Surely it was twice as heavy now? Her bag slung over her shoulder, she took a step forward, almost

7

bumping into a figure which had silently appeared.

'Don't you know this is private property?' demanded an imperious voice.

Laura looked at the tall, broad-shouldered man confronting her, noticing briefly the deep tan and glittering grey eyes. His hair, black and wiry, curled just below his ears. He was dressed in shabby grey trousers and navy sweater.

'I'm well aware of that.' Laura's green eyes flashed— a warning sign if he only knew it. 'As a matter of fact I'm Mr. Stuart's new secretary, so if you wouldn't mind telling me where I can find him—'

The grey eyes disconcertingly raked her from head to toe. Laura became conscious of her dishevelled appearance, her crumpled, mudstained skirt and laddered tights.

'*You* are Miss—er—Templeton?' He looked as if he could not believe his eyes.

'I am. If Mr. Stuart had had the good manners to send someone to meet me I shouldn't be in this state. Now perhaps you'll—'

'Just a minute, Miss Templeton. Mr. Stuart went himself to meet you.'

'In that case, why didn't I see him? I can assure you there was no one at the station.'

'That's right,' he answered grimly.

What did he mean? thought Laura. The man was talking in riddles. Who was he anyway—a gardener? What right had he to speak to her in such a high-handed manner?

'Would you mind explaining?' she said at last.

'You were due to arrive on Thursday. I made a special point of being there to meet you—wasting valuable time in the process. I think it's you who should be doing the

8

explaining.'

Quick colour flooded Laura's cheeks, her heart dropped. So this was Brad Stuart! Why hadn't he said so instead of letting her ramble on about his bad manners? And what did he mean, she should have been here on Thursday? Hadn't he himself suggested today? She set down her suitcase and searched in her handbag. 'I apologise if I've been rude, but I have your letter with me. I know you said today.'

'My dear Miss Templeton,' with ill-concealed impatience, 'I know exactly what I put in my letter to you. There's no need for that.' The thick dark brows were drawn together and he towered above her like an angry giant.

'Here you are,' she said at last, determined to prove her point. 'You'll see I'm right.'

His square brown hands deftly unfolded the sheet of notepaper and he scanned the page before thrusting it back. 'October the fifth,' he said shortly. 'Just as I thought.'

'B—but it can't be!' With the queerest feeling in the pit of her stomach Laura looked at the scrawling writing. Surely she hadn't been mistaken? Unhappily she realised that the figure did resemble a five, although she had taken it for an eight. 'Oh, dear.' She looked up apologetically. 'I'm sorry. I suppose I should have made sure—but I did sent a letter telling you which train I was taking.'

'Of course,' he jeered. 'Arriving at twelve, you said, but how about the date? Didn't you think to confirm that? The competent Miss Templeton! What a fool I was to believe David. He was obviously taken in by your pretty face and didn't mind whether you were efficient or not.' He eyed her slim, taut figure insolently, causing

Laura to retort:

'If that's your opinion I may as well go back to London!'

She picked up her case and turned away, but before she had taken more than a few steps felt a heavy hand on her shoulder. 'Miss Templeton, there are no more trains today. And judging by that limp you'll never reach the station. Let me take your case. My housekeeper will show you where you can tidy yourself and then perhaps we'll be able to discuss matters more rationally.'

His voice was softer, but his expression remained grim as he led the way, Laura following meekly in his wake. Suddenly the shrubs and trees thinned out and across a wide expanse of shining lawn Laura saw at closer quarters the house that David had lightly referred to as 'a rambling place in the country.'

It was a splendid Tudor-style building. The windows gleamed like molten gold in the afternoon sunshine and the black timbers stood out in sharp relief. As she looked at the gabled stone roof Laura glimpsed a face looking down from one of the windows. As quickly as it appeared it was gone and she was left with the feeling that perhaps it had been imagination.

Mr. Stuart opened the huge studded door, waiting impatiently for Laura to enter. The large hall was dim after the bright sunlight. Her shoes echoed on the marble floor. When her eyes became accustomed to the gloom she was unprepared for the elegant splendour of her surroundings. Exquisite pictures adorned the pale gold walls and an urn of beautifully arranged flowers stood in one corner. A curved staircase led to the upper regions and down these stairs now came a smiling woman in a plain black dress. Laura judged her to be in her early fifties. Small, neat, with a round, cheerful face, she was presumably the housekeeper.

The woman looked searchingly at Laura before speaking to her employer, who had put down Laura's suitcase and already had his hand on a door to their right. 'Mr. Anderson telephoned a few minutes ago. Said it was urgent and would you ring him back.' And then reproachfully, 'You didn't tell me you were expecting company, Mr. Stuart. Will the young lady be staying to tea?'

'I should imagine so, Jenny.'

For the first time Laura noticed a humorous twinkle in his eyes. So he wasn't always the forbidding character he made out.

'This is Miss Templeton—my housekeeper, Mrs. Jennings.'

For a second surprise registered on Mrs. Jennings' pleasant face, but she quickly pulled herself together. 'It's good to see you, miss. Shall I show Miss Templeton to her room, Mr. Stuart?'

'Please. Then we'll have tea in my study.' He disappeared behind the well-polished oak door. Mrs. Jennings picked up Laura's suitcase and crossed towards the imposing stairway.

'Let me carry that,' urged Laura. 'It's far too heavy for you.'

'I might look frail, but I'm very strong,' said the housekeeper over her shoulder. 'I thrive on hard work.'

They turned right at the top, along a narrow carpeted corridor. 'Here you are,' said Mrs. Jennings, opening a door. 'Your room's all ready, even though we thought you weren't coming.' Her voice dropped to a conspiratorial whisper. 'What happened to delay you? Mr. Stuart wasn't half cross.'

'I misread his writing, thought it was today I should come.' Laura smiled ruefully, realising instinctively that Mrs. Jennings could prove a useful ally should she decide to keep the job.

'Never mind. I expect he's glad you're here.'

If that's the case, thought Laura, he has a funny way of showing it. Aloud she said, 'You're probably right. What a beautiful room this is.' She touched the peach satin bedspread, noticing how perfectly it matched the walls. Gold velvet hung at the window and a thick oatmeal carpet covered the floor. 'Has Mr. Stuart always lived here?'

'Oh, no,' replied Mrs. Jennings, lingering in the doorway. 'About three years. Before that it was a Mr. Partridge and his wife, but they weren't like Mr. Stuart. Money makes no difference to him. He's a real gentleman. Treats me as though I was his mother most of the time.'

Laura was surprised to hear Mrs. Jennings' opinion of Brad Stuart. During the few minutes spent in his company she had found him thoroughly disagreeable. 'What happened to the Partridges? Why did they leave this beautiful house?'

'They moved down south. Wanted something better. Sold it just as it was, furniture, the lot.'

'Didn't they ask you to go with them?' Laura studied herself through the mirror, noticing with dismay her untidy hair and smudge across her forehead. No wonder Brad Stuart had doubted her identity.

Mrs. Jennings snorted disdainfully. 'They asked me all right, but Mrs. Partridge put it in such a way that I knew I wasn't wanted. So when Mr. Stuart asked me if I'd stay on, I jumped at the chance.'

'I'll say one thing for her,' said Laura, sliding her

fingers over the lustrous walnut top of the dressing table. 'She had good taste in furniture. Queen Anne, isn't it? I don't know much about antiques, but everything here looks the genuine thing.'

'Nothing but the best was good enough for her. But I mustn't stand chatting. The bathroom's next door. Come down when you're ready.'

The door clicked gently to and Laura sank on to a nearby chair. She felt utterly exhausted and not in the least like having tea with Brad Stuart. Looking around, she drank in the luxury of the room. This, she thought, was sheer heaven. It would be foolish to return to London because of a few words with her employer. There was no comparison between this and the dingy bedsitter she had left behind.

Crossing to the window, she looked out—beyond the lawns and trees surrounding the house, to the patchwork of fields in the distance, the faintly visible grey ribbon of road along which she had travelled. Comforted by the serenity of her surroundings, she slipped out of her crumpled suit and hunted through her suitcase for a tailored navy dress which would make her look much more like the efficient secretary she was supposed to be.

The bathroom was cool and green, and as Laura showered she felt some of the tension ease from her body. Perhaps she had been a trifle hasty in judging Brad Stuart? He had a perfect right to be annoyed when she was three days late, even though the fault was not strictly hers. She would have felt the same herself had the positions been reversed.

Brushing out her long auburn hair, which she had fastened up so carefully—was it only that morning?— she fastened it back into the customary knot she wore when working. She applied a mere touch of shadow to her eyes, carefully smoothed on coral pink lipstick, and when ten minutes later she presented herself in Brad Stuart's study looked smart and confident, even though her heart was pounding rapidly.

He sat at an enormous leather-covered desk, motioning her to sit as he continued writing. Cherry red curtains were draped at the windows through which Laura could see the Welsh hills rising majestically in the distance. The deep-piled carpet was in the same clear red. Books lined the walls and two well-worn armchairs were placed on either side of the marble fireplace, where logs burned cheerfully. The expensive smell of leather and Brad Stuart's cigar filled the room.

After several minutes Laura began to feel uncomfortable. Surely his writing could wait until after their discussion? It was difficult to believe Mrs. Jennings' statement that he was a gentleman. A gentleman would hardly keep her waiting, unless he was purposely trying to test her patience.

At this point in her thoughts the housekeeper entered and placed a tray on a low table beside Laura. 'Shall I pour, Mr. Stuart?'

'No, no, Miss Templeton will do it. Thank you, Jenny.

He looked at Laura through the rising smoke of his cigar. 'As you're my secretary I shall expect you to carry out small duties such as pouring tea, or even making it if Mrs. Jennings is out. There may also be isolated occasions when I wish to entertain and would want you to act as hostess.'

'I see.' Laura sat forward on the edge of her seat preparing to pour the tea. Unaccountably she felt pleased by his suggestion, even though he was taking it somewhat for granted that she intended staying despite her earlier outspoken words. Deep down she knew she wanted to stay. She loved the house already and would be a fool to turn down such a well-paid job.

One thing that did puzzle her was why his sister could not help him entertain. David had told her he lived with his sister, so it was reasonable to presume that she would be the one to stand at his side—not Laura, about whom he knew very little at that moment. Perhaps she would find out later, she decided, handing Brad Stuart his tea.

'You'll find it very quiet here after London.' He tilted back his chair, regarding her gravely. 'It's one of the reasons I like the place—although I know it's not everyone's choice. I can lose myself in my work without fear of interruption—except the infernal telephone. Naturally I shall expect you to take all calls from now on—only disturbing me if it's really necessary.'

Laura nodded. 'I understand, and I think I shall like it here. My parents kept a farm. It's one of the things I really miss.'

'Then why move to the city?' His eyes glinted cruelly. 'Or perhaps you were husband-hunting? Thought there'd be better prospects?'

Laura fought back her rising anger at his deliberate attempt to taunt her. If she wanted to keep the job she must keep a tight rein on her temper. 'To tell you the truth,' she said evenly, 'my parents were killed in a car accident. The farm went to my brother, but he sold it and flew to America. I decided to move to London, foolishly thinking that if I saved enough money I could buy the farm back one day. I was soon disillusioned. I used up what little money I had while at training college and when I eventually got a job it took all my salary to keep myself.'

'I see.' His face softened. 'Well, perhaps we'd better get to work. I'll explain briefly what I expect you to do.'

Laura listened attentively while studying his face. He really was extraordinarily handsome, she decided— probably in his early thirties. Dark, strong features, a well shaped, wide mouth, determined chin and those keen grey eyes which had lost their metallic glint for the moment. His deep voice was pleasant and soothing when he was not being dictatorial. She almost found herself liking him. If only she hadn't made that mistake things would have been different. As it was he hadn't much faith in her capabilities. It would be up to her to show him; to prove that David was right in his recommendation.

'And now,' Brad Stuart continued, 'if you've finished your tea I'll show you your office.' He opened a door in the wall behind him and waited for Laura to enter.

She looked in dismay at the small dark room. 'I can't work in here,' she said quietly.

'And why not? You've everything you need.' His brows met in a straight line.

Laura walked further into the room. 'B—but look at it!' An ancient typewriter sat on the littered desk. Handleless drawers were half open. The entire room had an air of neglect. None of the smart modern equipment she would have expected a famous author and wild life expert to possess. And what little light came through the tiny window did nothing to alleviate the gloom.

'I can't believe it. Did your last typist walk out on you?' His lips tightened and although he did not speak Laura knew she was right. 'It will take me a week to sort myself out.'

'That was the idea of you coming a few days early, Miss Templeton.'

Laura ignored the sarcasm. 'Where are the filing-cabinets? Surely not here?' Pulling open a huge wooden cupboard, she stared in fascinated horror as an avalanche of papers fell to the ground.

'I'm sorry, Mr. Stuart. I'll put these papers back, but I just cannot work under these conditions.' She hesitated as she saw his thunderous expression, but decided she might as well carry on. She had nothing to lose at this stage. 'I understand now why you can't keep anyone. It—it's impossible!'

'And just what do you suggest I should do?'

The scathing tones made Laura flinch, but she was determined to express her views. 'For a start I should need a bigger office, a room with more windows. Electric light's no good for your eyes all day. Then a proper filing-cabinet—and, of course, a new typewriter—preferably an electric one.'

She stopped. Mr. Stuart had closed the door and was leaning against it, listening, his head to one side.

'Do go on, Miss Templeton. No one's ever told me what I should do before.' His eyes were granite-hard and Laura swallowed the sudden constricting lump in her throat.

'I'm sorry if I've spoken out of turn, but now you'll realise why you've had difficulty with staff. If you don't mind, I'll go to my room. I think I'd better leave tomorrow after all.'

He made no offer to move and Laura stood awkwardly in front of him. She would have preferred to make a dignified exit after her outburst instead of being compelled to face him like a naughty schoolgirl.

'Now that you've had your say perhaps I can have

mine.' He folded his arms, regarding her coolly. 'It is the incompetence of so-called secretaries that has caused this chaos. If I could type I'd do the work myself, but I've no time or inclination to learn so I'm forced to depend on such as you. Am I to take it that the job's too much? That even with your experience you would be unable to cope?'

Mockery gleamed in his dark eyes, stinging Laura into retaliation. It was impossible to restrain her temper when he spoke to her in such a condescending manner. 'I have no doubt that I could cope, Mr. Stuart, even under such depressing conditions.'

He looked around, as if seeing the room for the first time. 'Perhaps it is somewhat small. I'd never really thought about it.' His voice unconsciously took on a pleading note, causing Laura to look at him sharply. 'Look, Miss Templeton, I have some work that must be sent off tomorrow. Would you help me out?'

Laura hesitated only a moment. There was no rush to return to London. If she was honest with herself she would admit that she did not really want to go back. If Brad Stuart was not so unsufferably rude she might even be able to put up with this poky office.

'Very well. Do you want me to start now?' She was almost sure she saw relief in his eyes, but the next moment, his face expressionless, he said in the authoritative tones she was beginning to expect:

'The rest of the day is yours. I shall expect you here at nine sharp in the morning. Breakfast is at eight in the dining-room. Mrs. Jennings will show you where it is.'

CHAPTER TWO

DETERMINED not to antagonise Brad Stuart any further, Laura rose early the next morning. At eight o'clock she entered the dining-room where she had eaten a solitary meal the evening before. Now the curtains were drawn back, allowing the sun's watery rays to fill the room. She crossed to the window through which she could see the shrub-lined drive along which she had trudged so wearily yesterday afternoon. Laura smiled. Everything seemed so different this morning. She had slept well and felt refreshed, ready to cope with any eventuality. Perhaps her employer, too, had overcome his ill temper and would treat her with a little more courtesy?

Turning to the table, she admired the crisp white linen and sparkling silver, but was surprised to note that again it was set for one. Laura sat down as Mrs. Jennings appeared with her breakfast. 'Here you are, love. I hope you slept well?'

'Wonderfully, thank you, Mrs. Jennings. Am I to eat alone? I expected Mr. Stuart and his sister.'

'Bless you no, miss,' replied the housekeeper, placing a plate of piping hot bacon and egg before Laura. 'Mr. Stuart eats in his study. Up at six, he was—says he works better in the early morning. As for Miss Helen, she has all her meals in her room.'

'It must make an awful lot of work for you. Why can't they eat in here?' It was inconsiderate to say the least of Brad Stuart and his sister to expect Mrs.

Jennings to run round after them, thought Laura crossly. Although from what little she had seen of her employer he seemed to live in a world of his own, preoccupied with his work to the exclusion of all else. Was his sister moulded along the same lines? she mused.

Mrs. Jennings shrugged. 'It's no concern of mine. Mr. Stuart pays me well, so I do as I'm told without any questions.'

It was a strange household, decided Laura, but she was inclined to agree with Mrs. Jennings that it was none of their business. Even so as she ate her breakfast she could not help but wonder how Helen Stuart spent her days. She recalled the fleeting face at the window. In view of Mrs. Jennings' statement it seemed logical to believe that it belonged to Brad's sister. Did she spend many hours in her room? There had certainly been no sign of her yesterday. It was as though they had the house to themselves. She wished now that she had asked David more about the occupants of Leastone Hall.

So immersed was Laura in thought that when Mrs. Jennings returned for her empty dishes she was surprised to note that it was already a quarter to nine. Dashing up to her room, she repaired her make-up, arriving in Brad Stuart's study at five minutes to nine.

He looked at his watch as she entered. 'Good morning, Miss Templeton. You're punctual today, I see.'

Laura bit her lip, wondering whether he would ever forget the incident. He had little hesitation in putting the blame on her, not once admitting that the fault could lie in his writing.

'Sit down a moment. I'm afraid the whole of my last book will have to be retyped. Miss Barber made such a mess of it.'

I'm not surprised, thought Laura, using such an

ancient typewriter. I can't understand him. There's no expense spared in the rest of the house, so why not make sure his secretary is well equipped? It doesn't make sense. Unless he genuinely hasn't given it a thought.

'Are you listening, Miss Templeton?' Her employer's voice broke into her reverie. 'I said there are one or two points I should like to go over with you where I may not have made myself clear.'

Standing beside him as he explained, Laura became acutely aware of the strength of his personality and knew that if they had met in different circumstances she would have found him exceedingly attractive. As it was, his biting tongue and aggressive manner only succeeded in annoying her. She was accustomed to courtesy and friendliness and his display of rudeness put her instantly on her guard.

She suddenly realised that he had finished speaking and was looking at her expectantly.

'You *do* understand? I know you have difficulty in reading my writing,' a slight pause, 'that's why I've gone through this with you. You'll get used to my scribble in time, but if you have any doubts do come and ask me.'

Laura nodded. 'It's perfectly clear, Mr. Stuart. I became quite expert at deciphering people's handwriting in my last job, so I don't anticipate any difficulty in reading yours.'

He raised an expressive eyebrow. 'Really! No one else seems able to transcribe my writing accurately. I even had my doubts about you—but we'll see. I have to go out now, but you'll find everything you need in the office.' He thrust the papers into Laura's hand, shrugged into his jacket and was gone.

Laura stood for a second at his desk, somehow loath to enter the gloomy office next door. It was not an inviting atmosphere in which to work. It would be much more pleasant sitting here, the warmth of the late autumn sunshine filling the room.

Outside a gardener was at work belatedly pulling up faded summer blooms in readiness for the spring bulbs. She would have dearly loved to spend the morning exploring the vast grounds. It was unusually warm and still. Birds chattered noisily in the nearby woods and the mountains of Wales struggled for supremacy through the distant mist.

Sighing deeply, Laura crossed to her office. If she wanted to make any headway before Brad Stuart returned she had better start.

Switching on the light, she ruefully surveyed the confusion of papers covering the desk, the overflowing waste-paper basket and the enormous pile that had fallen out of the filing-cupboard. Before she could get anything done it would be necessary to tidy up. It would be hopeless to try and work amongst such disorder.

The papers on the floor she pushed back into the cupboard—they could be sorted out and filed properly when she had time. The work on the desk appeared to be an assortment of unanswered letters and half-typed articles. Laura put them into a folder, intending to tackle Mr. Stuart about them later. How he made a success of his writing with such disorganisation she couldn't imagine, yet he must be wealthy to own such a magnificent estate.

Next she found her way to the kitchen. Gleaming copper pans hung on the timber-clad walls. There was nothing old-fashioned in here. Everything was laid out for Mrs. Jennings' convenience and Laura looked admiringly round before asking for polish and dusters.

'I hope you don't think I'm responsible for the state

of the office,' said Mrs. Jennings in concern, 'but Mr. Stuart point blank refused to let me in. Said he didn't want anything disturbed. He knew exactly where to find things as they were.'

Laura smiled. 'He'll be in for a shock if he wants anything now. I've put it all away. There's hardly room to swing a cat as it is. What made him choose a poky little hole like that to push his secretary into?'

'At one time he had her working with him.' Mrs. Jennings paused from rolling out pastry. 'But then he said the noise of the typewriter disturbed him so he had part of his study partitioned off. That's why there's only that tiny window. I don't suppose he thought of the poor girl's comfort so long as he wasn't disturbed. He's like a bear with a sore head if he's interrupted in the middle of a piece of work.'

'Didn't any of them ever complain?' asked Laura, silently agreeing with the housekeeper's philosophy. It tied in so completely with her own earlier views.

'Far from it. They all fell for his fatal charm. As far as I know he's a confirmed bachelor, but his typists have been so bewitched that I'm sure they would have worked in the attic if he asked them.' She gave a short laugh. 'When they realised it was no use they left—if he didn't sack them beforehand. I've seen it happen so many times—but I knew as soon as I saw you that you were different. This one won't put up with his domineering manner, I said to myself. She won't be afraid to speak her mind. And I'm right, aren't I?'

Laura laughed and nodded. She liked Mrs. Jennings and appreciated her forthright manner.

'You've got to stick up to him, Miss Templeton. He thinks more of you if you do. If I think I'm wronged I soon tell him, although I'm always careful to remember he's my boss. Jobs aren't easy to come by at my age.'

Laura placed her arm round the older woman's shoulders. 'You're a treasure, Mrs. Jennings, and I'm sure Mr. Stuart knows it. I must go now or he'll be back before I've started.'

At the door she turned. 'Mrs. Jennings—I'll have my lunch in here, if you like. I feel guilty about you having to lay a table just for me. Unless Mr. Stuart will be back?'

'No, miss. Said he was lunching out. As a matter of nose at the thought of eating in the kitchen with the fact it will be nice to have a bit of company, if you're sure you don't mind. Most people would turn up their housekeeper.'

With a warm smile Laura said, 'I shall look forward to it. What time will lunch be ready?'

'About one. I'll give you a call. Now off with you or there'll be nothing to eat at all.'

Laura soon had the office clean and tidy ready to begin the re-typing of her employer's book, but again she was held up. The keys of the typewriter needed cleaning and oiling. Laura searched in vain for oil and brushes, becoming more and more angry as the morning wore on. How did he expect her to turn out a decent page of typing on such a relic? It was a pity he couldn't type himself, then he would realise how much energy was used pounding away on the stiff old keys.

David had supplied her with an electric typewriter and her fingers had almost flown over the keys, each page being neatly and accurately presented. She took pride in her work, but it was impossible on this machine to type evenly when half the keys were out of alignment and the whole thing wanted overhauling. Or better still, said Laura to herself, throwing on to the scrap heap.

When Mrs. Jennings tapped on the door Laura had only typed the first half dozen pages, but even so felt exhausted and was glad of the respite.

'I'm fighting mad,' she said when they were seated at the huge wooden table in the centre of the kitchen. 'How does he expect me to use that heap of scrap metal? It's virtually impossible!'

'I've often wondered myself why Mr. Stuart kept that old machine,' said Mrs. Jennings. 'It isn't as though he couldn't afford a new one. He found it in the attic when he moved in. I think that's what gave him the idea of a secretary. He'd always sent his work away to be typed before.'

'And a better job they made of it, I'm sure,' replied Laura. 'But let's forget work for a while. It's a sore point. Tell me about Helen. Why doesn't she leave her room?'

'I'm not sure whether I ought to say, miss. Mr. Stuart doesn't like to talk about her. It's her legs, you see. She can't get about like she used to.'

Poor dear, thought Laura sympathetically, as she ate a mouthful of steak pie. 'Why doesn't he let her have a room down here? It would be better for you as well as her.'

'I'd rather not say, if you don't mind. Miss Helen's a forbidden subject in this household. I feel sorry for Mr. Stuart being burdened with her as he is, but that's as much as I'm going to say. How's the pie?'

'Delicious, thank you.' Laura could not understand the secrecy surrounding her employer's sister. It seemed that the woman was in need of company, not someone to be shut away upstairs. Perhaps if she asked Mr. Stuart he would let her see Helen. It was a shame for her to be alone.

Laura ate her last piece of potato. 'That was lovely, Mrs. Jennings. Do you do all the work in this house? Surely there's too much for one?'

'We have a daily, but I prefer to look after Mr. Stuart myself, and of course I'll do your room now—then I know it's been done properly. Most women are out for a bit of easy money these days and conveniently forget the corners. Peaches and cream?'

'No, thank you, just coffee. I won't feel like working if I eat too much.'

Halfway through the afternoon Brad Stuart returned. Laura heard him moving about in his study before he came to see how she was getting on.

Silently he stood at her desk scanning the pages. He took so long that Laura wondered whether she had done anything wrong.

At length he handed the papers back. 'They're fine, thank you, but I see you've only just started chapter two. I must have the first three chapters today. My publishers are breathing down my neck. I really thought that a woman of your experience would have rattled off three chapters by now with no trouble at all.'

His sarcasm was not lost on Laura and her voice was as cold as his. She was not going to take the blame for something that was not her fault. 'Mr. Stuart, you may not remember what a shambles this office was in, or care that it's hopeless to try and hurry on this—this museum piece.'

'Your typing looks all right to me, Miss Templeton. I can't see why you're complaining.' The steely grey eyes looked at her steadily.

'That's because I'm a good typist. Anyone with less experience would find it impossible to use. Even so, it's jolly hard work.'

He frowned briefly. 'I've never had a complaint before.'

'Perhaps if you had you might have done something about it.' It was impossible to control her temper when he spoke in such superior tones.

He gave her a last condemning look, choosing to ignore her statement, and strode from the room, saying over his shoulder, 'Leave the chapters on my desk when you've finished.'

For several minutes Laura sat still. He really was the most disagreeable person she had ever met! He might be her boss, but at least he could have a little consideration. It would take her hours to type two more chapters, and it wasn't as though the work was straightforward. There were so many alterations it was difficult to make out some of the words.

She was still brooding when Mrs. Jennings brought her a cup of tea and a biscuit. 'Never mind, love. Remember what I told you—he doesn't mean half what he says. In fact—I don't know whether I ought to tell you this, but it might cheer you up—he just told me that he's relieved to have found someone who can type properly. That, coming from the master, is praise indeed. So don't worry if he gets on to you. It's just his way.'

Cheered by Mrs. Jennings' words, but surprised that he should have discussed her with his housekeeper, Laura inserted a fresh piece of paper into her machine and started typing with more enthusiasm than she had previously felt. It was something that he appreciated her typing, although it would have been better to hear it from his own lips rather than second hand. She somehow suspected that he begrudged paying compliments, probably erecting this aggressive barrier to prevent her from following the path of her predecessors. He needn't worry, she liked her men with a little more respect for a woman.

It was late evening before she finished, and her arms and shoulders ached as though she had done a hard day's manual labour. Satisfied that the work had been done as neatly and accurately as circumstances permitted, Laura placed the pages on Brad's desk, allowing her eyes once more to take in the luxury of his room, her annoyance renewed at the inadequacy of her own quarters.

Wearily she closed the door. All she wanted now was a hot bath and the comfort of her bed. If Brad Stuart was going to work her this hard all the time she would earn every penny of the salary he was paying. It suddenly did not seem such a generous amount after all.

The next morning Brad was waiting when she entered his study, a sheaf of papers in his hand, a frown darkening his face. 'I'm afraid you've missed out a page, Miss Templeton. You'll have to re-type the last half of this chapter.'

Laura looked and found to her consternation that he was right, but it would be a simple matter to type out the page without re-doing the whole chapter.

'I'm sorry, I can't imagine how I missed it. But it won't be necessary to do it again. I can easily insert the missing page.'

'I prefer it re-typed,' he said determinedly, 'and you'll notice I've made one or two alterations—not your fault, but I think it sounds better.'

Furious, while maintaining an outward calm, Laura took the sheets into her office, spending half the morning angrily re-typing.

Her annoyance had spent itself when she took the work

back and she stood quietly by his desk as he quickly read it through.

'Yes, that's better,' he said at last. 'By the way, I've been looking for a letter from the *Weekly Review*. Apparently they wrote last month asking me to do an article on the wildebeeste as a follow-up to a recent television programme. I can't find it anywhere. You haven't seen it?'

It could be on her desk, thought Laura, but she had pushed all the letters together without looking to see who they were from. 'There's a whole pile of unanswered letters in my office. Perhaps it's amongst those.'

'You'd better bring them in. I don't know what they're doing there if they haven't been answered. Bring your pad as well. We'll go through them.'

When all the mail was signed and sealed Brad called Laura into his study, inviting her to sit down. His chin resting on the tips of his fingers he looked keenly at her for a long minute before speaking.

His words when he did speak took Laura very much by surprise.

'I'm sorry for the way I treated you when you arrived. You've proved that you're every bit as efficient as David said, despite the—er—inadequacy of your office.'

'Thank you, Mr. Stuart,' said Laura, feeling an unexpected warmth at his praise, but wondering whether he was merely buttering her up for something else.

Abruptly he stood up. 'Come with me. I want your opinion.'

Surprised, Laura followed. He led her into the room next to his study. It was comfortably furnished with deep armchairs and a chaise-longue in faded green velvet.

'Would this suit you?' His voice was brusque and businesslike.

'I'm sorry—I don't understand.'

'For your office. I could have this stuff moved out and a door put in here between the two rooms. What do you think?'

Laura could hardly believe him. It would be marvellous. It commanded the same breathtaking view as his own room and it was light and spacious. It would be a pleasure to work there. If she needed any incentive to stay, this was it. It would make up for all Brad Stuart's bad moods.

'It would be very nice, but—don't you use it?'

'Occasionally, if we have visitors. But that's very rare these days since my—' For a brief space his eyes shadowed. When he spoke again his voice was brisk. 'I'll call a man in tomorrow and you can move as soon as it's ready.'

Laura's thoughts were on Brad's unfinished sentence and she hardly heard his last words. What had he been going to say? Something about himself—or his sister? This latter seemed the most likely and Laura wondered if now was the time to question him or whether she should wait until she had settled in properly.

'Perhaps I'm jumping to conclusions, Miss Templeton? Perhaps you don't want to stay?'

Realising that Brad had mistaken her silence, Laura spoke hastily. 'Oh, no, I've made up my mind. I'll stay, after all.'

'Good. We're in agreement for once.' His face relaxed and Laura thought for one second that he was actually going to smile. But the next moment he left the room and she followed, not sure whether she was dismissed or not.

'There is one other point,' he said over his shoulder as they re-entered his study. 'I've had so many girls walk out on me that I should like to ensure it doesn't happen again. I've drawn up a contract for a period of three months which I would like you to sign.'

Laura drew in a deep breath. So she had been right— he did have an ulterior motive. It was not so much that she minded signing the contract, but the way he had gone about it. Softening her up before the crunch. Right, she said to herself grimly, two can play at that game! She smiled as she read through the contract, then with pen paused said:

'I'll sign on one condition.'

His eyebrows shot up, surprised, as if wondering how she dare suggest such a thing.

'And that is?'

He had adopted his old superior attitude, which only served to encourage Laura.

'That I have a new typewriter and proper filing-cabinets. I refuse to sit in that lovely room with—with that lot in there.'

Brad Stuart tilted back his chair—their eyes met and held. Then suddenly he smiled, displaying very white teeth in his brown face, a smile which dramatically changed him from a tyrant to a man. 'Very well, Miss Firecracker, you win. I see that to keep you I'll have to make you happy. We'll go into Shrewsbury in the morning and you can choose whatever you need.'

Because her victory was easier than she had anticipated Laura felt no elation, merely thanking him before going to her room to shower and change for dinner. The man was an enigma. She had fully expected him to turn on

her, to question her audacity. But to laugh and agree—
it was the last reaction she had counted on. It showed a
side to his character yet unknown—a side she could
learn to like!

Mrs. Jennings on the other hand was very amused
when Laura told her about their conversation. 'I can
just imagine his face when you told him! No one's ever
dared speak like that before, except me, of course. I can
get anything out of him. He's not so masterful as he
makes out—just a little thoughtless. His work is so much
on his mind that he hasn't the time for anything else.'

'I expect you're right,' said Laura absently. She was
remembering the smile that had transformed his face.
Despite his ability to bring out the worst in her she was
not immune to his attractions, even though there was no
chance of her falling in love with him. David was her
sort of person—kind, considerate and patient—a complete contrast to Brad Stuart with his overbearing
superiority.

Brad appeared in the dining-room almost before Laura
had finished her breakfast the next morning. 'The car's
outside. Are you ready?'

'Just give me a minute to collect my coat,' she replied,
gulping down the last mouthful of coffee and wiping
her mouth on a napkin, knowing instinctively that he
was not the sort of person who liked to be kept waiting.

He was revving up the engine when she slipped into
the seat beside him, immediately easing the gleaming
silver Jaguar along the drive on to the open road.

Glancing at her curiously, he asked, 'Is driving one
of your talents, Miss Templeton?'

'Yes,' replied Laura cautiously, not wishing to be

drawn into retaliation by the caustic tones of his voice. 'I do drive, although I've never possessed a car of my own.'

'There's a Mini in the garage—you can use it if you like. The bus service is atrocious, as you probably found out the day you arrived.' His voice was suddenly friendly and Laura smiled.

'Thank you, but I hope to do some walking while I'm here, even if I am a little out of practice.'

'Oh, yes, I'd forgotten you were a country girl. Who knows, I may join you one of these days. I enjoy a good tramp.'

Surprised, Laura said, 'That would be very nice,' if a little disconcerting, she added to herself. He was dangerously attractive in this friendly mood and even though love was out of the question his presence was disturbing. She felt oddly breathless and scolded herself for allowing a few kind words to have this effect, especially after the way he had previously treated her.

Silence fell between them and for the rest of the journey Laura was content to relax and enjoy the passing scenery. She had been too annoyed on her journey here to take much notice of her surroundings but now was able to appreciate the beauty of the countryside in which she found herself. The delightful patchwork of fields, the trees in varying shades of green and gold. It was all very beautiful and a far cry from the concrete jungle that had been her home for the last six years.

When they reached Shrewsbury her employer stopped outside a large modern office equipment shop. 'I'll leave you to choose. You probably have a better idea than me.'

Laura looked at him wide-eyed. 'But I don't know

how much you're prepared to spend.'

He smiled, grey eyes crinkling kindly at the corners. 'Don't worry about money. Have it charged to my account, Fit the office out completely. I don't want you getting on to me again.' A slight pause as his eyes twinkled. 'I have other business to attend to now, but I'll pick you up here at twelve-thirty and we'll go somewhere for lunch.'

He was gone, leaving Laura open-mouthed on the pavement, hardly able to credit that this was the same man who had greeted her so rudely two days ago. The change in him was unbelievable, so out of character with her pre-formed opinion. It seemed that Jenny was right after all : with the right handling he was indeed a 'real gentleman'. She hoped this mood of affinity would last—it would make her job so much more pleasant. There was nothing worse than working in a discordant atmosphere.

The salesman who greeted her was most helpful, but afraid in case Mr. Stuart rated her for overspending, Laura chose with care two filing-cabinets, a desk and chair and, with her heart in her mouth, the latest in electric typewriters. She also ordered a small stationery cupboard and a supply of stationery, which she had noticed was very low.

Before long she had finished. She still had two hours to spare, so she wandered in and out of the shops buying tights and make-up and a few magazines. At twelve she stopped for coffee in a charming old-world restaurant she discovered in a narrow back street.

In her corner Laura felt suddenly lonely. The other tables were occupied by groups of people, laughing and talking, reminding her of when she first moved to

34

London. She had hated it until eventually she had made friends.

'May I join you?' Startled, she saw Brad smiling down. 'I finished earlier than I expected and came in here to kill time. It was a welcome surprise to see you —but you look very sad. You're not having second thoughts?' He pulled out a chair, his grey eyes regarding her with amusement.

'Just feeling lonely.'

'My fault. I shouldn't have left you so long. I'd forgotten you were a stranger to the town.' His voice was low and kind and Laura looked at him, wondering what had caused this unusual solicitude.

'I'm not blaming you,' she said huskily, her green eyes wide and slightly embarrassed. 'I enjoyed wandering round the town.'

Beckoning a waitress, he said, 'Now we're here we may as well have lunch. They do a jolly good veal and ham pie. How does that sound?'

'Fine. I'm starving.'

Laura noticed the heads that turned to look at her handsome escort. He was obviously well known and she enjoyed the envious glances slanted in her direction. He seemed an entirely different person today and for the first time since leaving London she felt completely happy.

Once outside in the mild autumn sunshine, Brad said, 'How about making a day of it, Laura?'

He seemed not to notice the use of her Christian name and Laura's spirits rose even higher. She smiled happily up into his face, green eyes meeting grey in a spirit of comradeship.

'You should congratulate yourself,' he said, adjusting his stride to fit hers. 'It isn't very often anyone gets me away from work.'

'Then I'm glad I have,' said Laura. 'You know what they say about all work and no play.'

They strolled through absurdly narrow streets, sometimes charming, sometimes sordid. Laura exclaiming delightedly over old names such as Grope Lane, Shoplatch, Dogpole. They admired the Dingle, a sun-trap garden with a lake at the bottom which Brad explained had once been a quarry, and where the famous Shrewsbury flower show was held every year. And finally they wandered along the river bank, drinking in the tranquillity of the late afternoon.

To Laura the whole day held an aura of unreality. It was inconceivable to associate this charmingly, attentive man with her tyrant of a boss, and when they started their homeward journey she sank back contentedly into her seat, saying:

'Thank you for a wonderful day, Mr. Stuart.'

'Brad, please.'

'Thank you—Brad. I can't imagine why I ever thought I'd like London. Today has brought back nostalgic childhood memories.'

He slanted her a quick glance. 'There's plenty to explore round here, but you'd better make the most of it before winter. It's not unknown for us to be snowbound for several days at a time.'

Laura closed her eyes, resting her head on the top of the seat. 'Snow in the country—so white and pure, transforming the trees and fields into fairyland.'

Brad's laugh rang out, filling the car and causing her to turn quickly.

'Why, you're nothing but a little girl at heart,' he grinned. 'Despite the outward sophistication.'

'Don't we all retain some of our childhood fancies?' she laughed back. 'Even if we're afraid to admit it?'

'I suppose so,' he said thoughtfully, and the frown remained on his face for most of the journey.

Laura would have dearly liked to ask what he was thinking, but even though their relationship had taken huge steps forward she felt that such a question would be regarded as an impertinence.

At last Leastone Hall came into sight and as he turned into the drive Brad said, 'So endeth a most enjoyable day. If anyone had told me a week ago that I'd be exploring Shrewsbury today with my secretary I'd have called them a liar. You're a remarkable young woman—do you know that?'

Laura shook her head, slightly bewildered. She could not imagine what was remarkable about her. It had been his idea to spend the day together.

His laugh was easy. 'You don't know me very well yet. I haven't had a day out like this in years.'

The Jaguar's tyres screeched to a halt on the gravel at the front of the house. Before Laura had time to open her door he caught her hand.

'Thank you, Laura,' he said simply.

The pressure was light, but Laura felt a sudden quickening of her pulses and flushed as she saw the warmth in his eyes. In confusion she pulled her hand free, jumping quickly out of the car, not daring to look back.

In the seclusion of her room, she scolded herself for behaving childishly. 'He must think me frightfully naïve,' she said aloud, 'acting so foolishly over a simple gesture. It isn't as if I'm in love with him.' His other secretaries might have fallen for his undeniable good

looks and admirable physique, but not Laura Templeton. Oh, no! Today had revealed an unsuspected charm,
but she knew the sort of man he really was. The
arrogant, domineering man. The man who had to be
master. Not at all the sort of person who would appeal
to her.

CHAPTER THREE

ONE look at Brad's face when Laura entered his study the next morning told her that the easy friendship of yesterday had gone. He was frowning deeply over a batch of papers and scarcely gave her a civil greeting.

She passed quietly through into her own office, took the dustcover from her typewriter and carried on with his book.

Ten minutes later she jumped violently as Brad boomed out, 'Miss Templeton, bring me the Anderson file!'

She searched hastily through the papers in the cupboard, but although she found a blue folder bearing the name no papers were inside, nor could she find any after a further search through the disordered contents.

'Miss Templeton!' the voice roared again.

Laura walked in, showed him the empty folder, inwardly seething at being called in such a peremptory fashion, and said, 'I'm sorry, but the letters are missing. They must be somewhere in the cupboard. I've had a quick look—but it's in such a mess.'

'Then sort it out, girl. What do you think I employ you for? Bring me Anderson's correspondence as soon as you find it.'

Dismissed, Laura returned to her office. It would take ages to sort out all those papers. Far better to do it when the new cabinets were delivered. Otherwise there was the danger of them falling out again, and hadn't he said his book was of prime importance at the moment?

Systematically searching, she soon found the Anderson papers, but when she took them in he did not even bother to look up, merely grunting his acknowledgement.

Why should I care? Laura asked herself crossly. Let him be disagreeable. I'll show him that it doesn't matter. I'm here to do a job and so long as I do it well that's all I've got to worry about.

The next two days passed in uneasy silence on Laura's part, whereas Brad was so involved in his writing that he appeared not to even notice her presence. Except, of course, when he wanted something—then he was either icily polite or belligerently rude.

Laura was glad when Saturday arrived. Two days in which to do as she liked. She allowed herself the luxury of an extra hour in bed, then over breakfast asked Mrs. Jennings to pack her a picnic lunch. She intended spending her weekend exploring the surrounding countryside.

By Monday morning she felt refreshed and well able to cope with any demands Brad made. The first thing she noticed as she entered his room was that a door had been put into the wall connecting it to the room which was to be her office.

'It's all ready,' he smiled, observing her quick glance. 'The furniture arrived on Saturday. I commend your choice.'

Laura was pleased to have met with his approval, but wished he had told her about it so that she could have stayed in and moved her own papers and equipment instead of wasting time this morning.

He crossed and opened the door, standing back for her to enter, an enigmatic smile on his face. Puzzled, Laura stepped into the room, halting abruptly when she saw that everything was ready—down to the last paperclip.

Brad chuckled and she turned on him accusingly. 'Why didn't you say? I'd have stayed to help. The man in the shop said the furniture wouldn't be delivered until this week.'

'I know, but I phoned and asked them to bring it on Saturday. I shall be out for the rest of the week and I wanted it settled before I leave. Everything's been transferred, except for the letters in the filing-cupboard. It will be a mammoth task sorting that lot out, but I've no doubt you will cope.' He returned to his desk. 'Did you enjoy your weekend?'

He was still smiling and Laura wondered at the change in him. It seemed that when he was involved on a particular project he had no time for anyone else, but when the work was finished he suddenly realised that he was living among normal human beings who appreciated the courtesies of life. Whatever it was, his awareness of her capabilities caused a warm glow to spread inside her and she found herself excitedly telling him of the villages and churches she had explored, and how wonderful the countryside was around Leastone Hall.

When she had finished he said, 'We must explore these wonderful places together one day, Laura. You shall be my guide—but now,' he picked up a sheaf of papers, 'I must rush. Here's a number of articles that I want typing this week. You've nearly finished my book?'

'Y-yes—only two more chapters.' Her heartbeats had quickened at the thought of another day out in his company, but quickly she pulled herself together. Surely she wasn't falling for his charms? It was impossible. When she fell in love it would have to be someone like David—charming, kind and positively not temperamental. How could anyone live with Brad when he was in one of his moods? He might be famous, but at what cost to his family and friends had his books been written? After only a week she was beginning to dread approaching him when he was at work, though why he should be so bad-tempered she could not imagine. Were all authors the same?

Suddenly she noticed that Brad was watching her curiously. 'Is there anything wrong?' he asked. 'You've been looking at me very strangely for the last half minute.'

Her cheeks flushed as she realised how rude he must think her. 'No, nothing. I'm sorry, I didn't mean to stare.'

'That's all right.' He smiled warmly. 'I shall be in Bristol until Friday—I'm giving a series of lectures. Here's my number in case you need me.' He turned at the door, eyes twinkling. 'I'll leave everything in your capable hands, Laura. I'm sure you won't be able to complain about your working conditions now?'

Laura smiled her thanks, sitting for a while at her desk after he had gone. He had positioned it so that as she worked she could admire the view from the window. How thoughtful, thought Laura happily. Now I shall be able to watch the changing shades of autumn. And later the frosts and snows.

Already the leaves were turning yellow. Before long they would fall and the lawns would be carpeted in brown and gold. As she watched a gust of wind enticed a handful of leaves from the trees and they danced merrily across the grass before being caught in a yew hedge a few yards further on.

Turning her attention back to her typewriter, Laura forced herself to concentrate on the task of finishing

Brad's book. Much as she loved the great outdoors work had to come first.

It seemed no time at all before Mrs. Jennings came in with her mid-morning coffee and by lunch time she had finished one chapter and was half way through the second. As on the previous occasion when Brad was out Laura lunched with Mrs. Jennings, but hurried back to her office immediately afterwards as she wanted to finish the book and make a start on the articles.

She was able to work much quicker with her new typewriter and by Tuesday evening all the typing was done. On Wednesday she settled down to the enormous task of sorting out the files, but this, too, proved easier than she had at first felt and by mid-morning on Thursday the work was finished. She was left wondering how to occupy herself for the rest of the week.

When she mentioned her dilemma to Mrs. Jennings she was told, 'Take the time off, love. Mr. Stuart can't tell you off for not working if there's nothing to do. Why don't you go for a walk? It's a lovely afternoon.'

'Oh, I couldn't.' Laura looked horrified. 'I mean, someone might telephone or Mr. Stuart might ring, then what would he say if I wasn't here to take a message? I couldn't possibly leave the house.'

'As you like,' retorted Mrs. Jennings, looking as if she thought Laura was silly not to take advantage of the situation. 'Anyway, it's my afternoon off, so you'll have the house to yourself—more or less.'

Laura guessed that she was referring to Helen and after the housekeeper had left could not help but wonder about the woman who confined herself to one room. Why did she shut herself away so completely from the rest of the household? Why had Brad never mentioned his sister? It was a strange state of affairs and the more

43

Laura considered it the more curious she became.

She tried to read, but it was difficult to forget that the only other person in the house was someone she had never met, nor was likely to meet by the look of things. Laura had been unable to pluck up courage to ask Brad about his sister and it was obvious that he was not going to volunteer any information. With sudden determination she decided to find out for herself.

At the top of the staircase she paused. Her own room lay to the right, but if the face she had seen at the window did belong to Helen it would mean that her room was somewhere along the corridor on her left, a part of the house she had never seen before.

There was no response from the first three rooms and when Laura opened the doors she saw that the furniture was shrouded in dust sheets. Behind the fourth door Laura thought she heard a noise, although there was no reply to her knock. After a few seconds she knocked again, then gently opened the door.

The room was exquisitely furnished in shades of pink and grey. For a moment Laura thought that she had been mistaken, that the room was empty. Then, in the shadows by the window, where a blind had been drawn to shut out the sunlight, she saw a still figure sitting in an armchair.

The occupant gave no indication that she was aware of Laura's presence and Laura herself hesitated, wondering whether to speak or silently retreat. She had just decided on the latter when a friendly voice said, 'Do come in and let me have a look at you. I presume you are Laura Templeton? Brad's told me so much about you.'

Laura was unaware that Brad visited his sister very often and was amazed to hear that they had discussed her. This put a different light on her conception that Helen and Brad were not very well disposed towards one another, and as she closed the door she looked curiously at the other woman.

It was difficult in the dim light to distinguish her features, but Laura could see the slim, well-shaped body, and the dark shoulder-length hair.

'Draw up the blind,' commanded the deep, husky voice. 'I want to see you more clearly.'

Laura obeyed, gasping incredulously as she turned away from the window and saw Helen clearly for the first time.

She had gained the impression that Helen was considerably older than Brad, and was astonished to see an exceedingly beautiful girl about her own age.

Helen laughed drily. 'What's the matter? Aren't I what you expected? I know Brad doesn't like discussing me, but I wasn't aware that he gave people the idea that I was something out of the ordinary.'

'Oh, no, not at all. It's just that I thought you would be much older.'

Helen raised her finely shaped brows, grey eyes so much like her brother's wide and disbelieving. 'He led you to believe that?'

With heightened colour Laura replied, 'Not exactly. In fact Brad—er—Mr. Stuart has never mentioned you. It was Mrs. Jennings—she said you suffered with your legs and I imagined an old lady with rheumatics or something.'

Helen's laugh rang out—this time a laugh of sheer amusement. 'At least you're honest. Pull up a chair. I think I'm going to like you, Miss Templeton. Or may I call you Laura?'

'Please do. I'm sorry if I stared.' Laura fetched a

basket chair from beside the lace-covered bed and sat down opposite Helen.

'Tell me,' said Helen, 'what made you decide to visit me? A genuine interest in old ladies or curiosity to see why I've become a recluse?'

'Curiosity, I suppose,' replied Laura carefully, 'and concern that you should shut yourself away. It doesn't seem right living here all alone.'

'What choice have I?' Helen's voice was all at once irritable and the jerky movements of her hands indicated a tension not otherwise apparent. 'This is Brad's house and he insists I stay in this room. I'm not surprised he hasn't told you about me. He never lets me see anyone. He can't bear illness in any shape or form and although he visits me every day I know he regards it as a duty rather than a pleasure.'

What an unfeeling man, thought Laura crossly. How could he treat his own sister like that? Impulsively she leaned forward, clasping the other girl's beautifully manicured hands in her own. 'At least I'll come and see you, and if you think it will do any good I'll have a word with Mr. Stuart suggesting you spend part of your day downstairs.'

'You mustn't do that.' Helen snatched away her hands abruptly, her previous well-modulated tones harsh with annoyance. 'Brad would never allow such a thing, and if he finds out you've visited me he'll be very angry.'

'I can't see why,' said Laura, puzzled. 'It's inhuman to expect you to remain here. It would drive me mad looking at the same four walls day after day.'

'That's how I feel sometimes,' said Helen softly. 'If only I could walk, escape from this—this prison!'

Moved to sympathy, Laura asked gently, 'Your legs, Helen—what's the matter with them?'

'I was in a car accident.' The words were scarcely audible and Laura leaned forward to hear what she was saying. 'The doctors say I'll never walk again.'

Her lips trembled and Laura laid a comforting hand on her arm. 'Have you never considered using a wheelchair?'

Helen nodded, her eyes moist. 'But Brad wouldn't hear of it. He couldn't bear to see me around him—a perpetual reminder of what happened.'

'What a heartless brute he is,' said Laura feelingly, privately determined to have a word with him. He deserved to be told in no uncertain terms what a merciless, cold-hearted person he was. It was unforgivable to treat his sister like this. How would he feel if the positions were reversed? Not very happy, she guessed. No one would. Helen was right when she referred to it as a prison. It was like being in solitary confinement, paying penance for something that was not her fault.

As Laura lay in bed that night she wondered why Helen did not face up to Brad, insist she was allowed more freedom. How long had the poor girl been imprisoned in her room? Weeks, months, maybe years? It was incredible to believe that Brad was capable of such callousness. Had he ever stopped to think of the future? Helen couldn't stay there for ever—growing old and stagnant like a cabbage. It was enough to drive anyone insane. She would tackle Brad as soon as he returned, make him see how wrong he was and insist Helen be allowed downstairs with company of her own age.

The next morning, after she had sorted the mail, she once again slipped upstairs to Helen's room. This time her knock was answered. Helen sat up in bed, a froth of pink lace round her shoulders, a touch of blue shadow emphasising the clear grey of her eyes, her lips outlined with vivid pink lipstick. Smiling, she patted the bed. 'I hoped you'd come. Sit here. It's been so long since I had anyone to talk to apart from Jenny and Brad I feel quite excited.'

Laura crossed the room, her feet sinking into the luxurious grey carpet. 'What do you do with yourself all day? You must find it terribly boring.'

'I do,' Helen grimaced. 'I spend most of the morning reading newspapers and magazines, then later Brad helps me to my chair by the window—although there's not much to see.' Her voice grew peevish. 'No one bothers to come now I'm a cripple. I used to throw weekend parties for my friends from London. But now —no one wants to know me.'

How tragic, sympathised Laura, that this beautiful creature was condemned to a life of inactivity. She was more determined than ever to try and make Brad understand the futility of keeping Helen away from other people. Signs of bitterness were already apparent and this would increase over the years until she became a complaining, disillusioned old woman. Resolutely Laura made up her mind to do all in her power to prevent this from happening.

'At least you have me,' she said. 'I'll come and see you as often as I can, although Mr. Stuart keeps me pretty busy.'

'What's it like—working for Brad?' asked Helen, picking up a hand mirror and studying her flawless complexion. 'I expect he treats you terribly, as he does me?' She observed Laura closely, waiting for her reply, almost as if the other girl's answer was important to her.

Laura chose her words with care. 'He's not a bad boss. He expects a high degree of efficiency, but so long as he gets that he's satisfied.'

'And what do you think of him as a man?' Helen's eyes sparkled. 'He told me that all his other secretaries imagined themselves to be in love with him.'

Laura's heartbeats quickened as she recalled the feel of his hand on hers, the delightful anticipation she had experienced at the thought of another day out with him, but she deliberately kept her face expressionless. 'So I believe. What has he told you about me?'

Helen laughed. 'Confidentially, he says you're a spitfire. He blames it on your hair—I think it's a gorgeous colour—but really, I think he enjoys the conflict, in contrast to all those other weak-willed girls who scurried round like mice at his slightest word.'

'I pity the poor girl he marries,' said Laura. 'Besides loving him she'll need to have the patience of Job, the diplomacy of a politician and a sense of humour to see her through all the bad times.'

'You don't see yourself in that role?' asked Helen bluntly.

'Definitely not. He's far too domineering. I'm not the sort who'd make a meek, submissive wife.'

'Pity. I'd enjoy having you as a sister-in-law.'

At that moment Mrs. Jennings entered with coffee for the two girls. Laura was thankful for the interruption as the conversation had become a little too personal for her liking. She had felt suddenly breathless at the thought of Brad, but was at a loss to understand why.

'I thought I'd find you here,' said the housekeeper. 'Miss Helen told me you visited her yesterday. I hope the master doesn't find out. He gave me instructions that I was to let no one up.'

'Surely he won't mind me?' responded Laura anxiously. 'I think it's jolly unkind of him to keep

49

Helen here like this. If I had my way I'd—'

'Now, now, miss,' interrupted Mrs. Jennings. 'We all know what he's like. What he decides is his own business. We're paid to do a job and we mustn't interfere in his private life.'

'I suppose you're right,' conceded Laura reluctantly. 'But it doesn't alter the fact that I think he's heartless and cruel. If he were my brother I'd make sure he didn't treat me like he treats Helen.'

Helen smiled indulgently. 'If you have to rely on him for a home you'd learn to accept his rules.'

Mrs. Jennings retreated, turning at the door to ask: 'Will you be wanting your lunch in here, Laura?'

'Please. If it's not too much trouble and Helen doesn't mind.'

'Of course not. It will make a welcome change.' The dark curls bounced as Helen shook her head.

'Would you like me to help you out of bed?' asked Mrs. Jennings next.

'I'll stay here today, Jenny. Now I've got someone to talk to I don't mind.'

'As you wish, Miss Helen.' Mrs. Jennings clucked disapprovingly, but Helen laughed as she closed the door.

'I'm glad you're here, Laura. Otherwise she'd have made me get up. She says I must try and use my legs, even though she has to drag me into the chair. Silly old woman,' she added disrespectfully.

Laura decided it was time to change the subject. She was very fond of the housekeeper and did not like to hear the other girl speak of her in such disparaging tones.

'What did you do before your accident, Helen? Did you live here then?'

'Oh, no.' The grey eyes were animated. 'I lived in

London. I came home weekends, but you see, I was an actress.' She thrust back her head in a theatrical gesture. 'Not a very well known one, I admit, but I was beginning to make a name for myself. Mummy wanted me to be a ballet dancer like herself, but I'd set my heart on the theatre. When she died I gave up dancing altogether, much to Brad's disgust.'

'Surely it didn't concern him?'

'He felt responsible for me. Our father died when we were small and as we grew up Brad tried to take his place.' She pulled a long face. 'He said I was letting down the family name. But there wasn't much he could do about it—I was eighteen and well able to take care of myself. We've never really seen eye to eye since. That's probably why he's so horrible towards me now.' She pouted prettily.

Laura, shocked that Helen's career should have been cut off so abruptly, said, 'Surely if you're good enough they could find you sitting-down parts? It would be better than nothing.'

A glimpse of something like horror appeared on the other girl's face, but it was gone instantly to be replaced by self-pity. 'Brad would never let me. It would humiliate him to think that other people could see me—like this, utterly helpless. Put my cup on the table, there's a darling. I think I'll have a sleep before lunch.' She passed a weary hand across her forehead. 'I feel so tired all of a sudden. It must be because I'm not used to visitors.'

Laura spent the next hour walking in the grounds, kicking her feet through the drifts of leaves that had now fallen. She was puzzled by the expression she had seen on Helen's face, convinced that tiredness had been an excuse to get rid of her. There was something she still did not know, and the more she thought about it the more puzzled she became. She was not surprised, therefore, when Mrs. Jennings told her later that Helen had refused lunch and did not want to be disturbed for the rest of the day.

Contrary to her previous decision not to leave the house when she should be working, Laura decided to take the Mini into Shrewsbury and do some shopping. It would take her mind off Helen and she could buy some wool to knit herself a thick sweater for the winter. The weather was already getting too cold to venture out of doors after dinner and it would help fill in the long evenings.

It did not take her long to finish her shopping and afterwards she went into the same little restaurant where she had eaten with Brad—was it really only a little over a week ago? It seemed as though she had been living at Leastone Hall for much longer.

As she sipped her coffee, savouring the strong, aromatic flavour, Brad's familiar voice reached her ears. At first she thought she must be mistaken. He wasn't due back until this evening. It was probably someone else with a similar inflection. Then she saw him—giving an order in his deep, authoritative tones to a blushing waitress.

Almost as though he was aware of her eyes on him he looked up, smiling as he recognised his secretary, beckoning her to join him.

'We seem to make a habit of meeting here,' he said, as she placed her coffee cup on the table. 'I see you've been doing some shopping.'

'Y-yes.' Laura felt embarrassed at being caught out by her employer when she should have been working. 'I'd finished your typing and I wanted a few things, so

I thought I'd—I'm sorry if—'

'There's no need to apologise.' He looked kindly at her. 'I'm not complaining. Your time's your own when I'm not there. I know you wouldn't play truant if there was work to be done. Would you care to join me for a meal?'

Relieved by his attitude, Laura smiled, unaware of the attractive picture she made. The cool wind had brought a healthy glow to her cheeks and her beautiful green eyes sparkled as she replied, 'Thank you—no, I haven't long eaten. But do carry on. I shall be going in a minute.'

'Oh no, you won't,' he said firmly. 'You can stay here, then we'll drive home together. I could do with your company right now. It's been a tiring week.'

'But the Mini—it's in the car park.'

'Then it can stay there. I'll send Jarvis for it tomorrow.'

The waitress brought Brad's meal and they were silent for a while as he hungrily did justice to the gammon and pineapple.

He then ordered another coffee for Laura and one for himself. Laura wondered whether now was the time to speak to him about Helen, while he was in such a good humour. Before she could speak, however, he started telling her about the talks he had given that week. He had never discussed his work with her before and she found it very interesting. His voice seemed to hypnotise her and she sat as if in a trance, even after he had finished.

Suddenly he nudged her arm. 'Come back, Laura. It's time to go.' He gathered up her parcels and she hurried by his side to the Jaguar which was parked a few yards away.

They drove in silence for a few minutes, then when they were out of the busy streets Laura gathered up her courage to say, 'Why haven't you told me about Helen? I would have gone to see her before if I'd known how much she craved company.'

Laura sensed his sudden withdrawal and clenched her fists tightly as she waited for his reply. When at last he spoke his voice was distant. 'You've been to see Helen?'

'Y-yes. We had quite a talk.' She tried hard to keep her voice natural, realising that Brad was annoyed and that the earlier easy friendship had disappeared.

'And may I ask who gave you permission?' Once again he was the master, and Laura felt her blood begin to boil.

'I wasn't aware I needed permission. I felt sorry for her all alone in that great house and decided to find out for myself why she stayed in her room.'

'And?' His voice was icy as he slanted a cutting glance in her direction.

'I found out that it's *you* who won't let her come down.' Laura's voice rose passionately. 'You keep her up there, deny her any visitors. How can you treat her like that? Are you ashamed of her because she can't walk?'

Brad swung the car into the side of the road, killed the engine, and turned towards her.

'Miss Templeton, I don't really see that it's any concern of yours what goes on in my house, but as you've found it necessary to interest yourself in my affairs I think you'd better know the truth.'

Laura faced him bravely. 'I do know the truth. I have no reason to disbelieve anything your sister has told me. If you think you're going to put yourself right in

54

my eyes you're mistaken.'

He nodded slowly. 'Talent gone to waste. She's still a good actress.'

Laura frowned, puzzled. 'What do you mean? What has her acting to do with the present situation?'

'Nothing—nothing at all.' His voice was tired now, as if he was weary of the whole affair.

He restarted the engine and during the silence that followed Laura recalled Helen's horrified look at her suggestion she carry on acting. In view of Brad's reaction it would seem she had been mistaken in feeling sorry for Helen. He had more or less insinuated that Helen had been acting. If this was so it could throw a different light on to the story, but she couldn't possibly ask Brad now—not after she had refused to listen to him. One look at his grim face told her that the subject was closed. She would have to try and find out for herself exactly what was going on in this strange household.

CHAPTER FOUR

AFTER dinner Laura settled in front of a blazing log fire in the comfortable lounge where she had become accustomed to spending her evenings. She had bought some vivid green wool and was looking forward to starting her jumper.

She had seen no more of Brad since they reached home. He had not appeared at dinner and no light shone from beneath his study door. It was her guess that he was upstairs with Helen—probably telling her off for allowing Laura to visit her.

Suddenly the door opened and Mrs. Jennings burst in. 'Mr. Stuart wants to see you. In Miss Helen's room.' She bit her lip worriedly. 'I hope you're not in trouble.'

'Don't worry, Jenny,' smiled Lauura with more confidence than she felt. 'I've already told him about seeing Helen. Perhaps he's decided he would like me to visit her after all.'

Jenny's brow cleared. 'I hope you're right. Mind you don't keep him waiting, now.'

Laura packed her knitting into a bag at the side of her chair and followed the housekeeper into the hall. Upstairs raised voices came from Helen's room. About to knock she heard her own name mentioned and involuntarily halted.

'I don't care what you thought. You had no right to lie to Miss Templeton,' Brad said with some asperity. Laura held her breath, waiting for Helen's reply. She knew she ought not to listen, but there was something about hearing herself discussed that rooted her to the spot.

When Helen did speak her voice held a whining, unpleasant tone, in complete contrast to the soft, husky pitch she had used when speaking to Laura.

'I didn't want her to know that I can't bear the thought of anyone seeing me like this—that's why I said you kept me here. Oh, I wish I was dead, and you can tell your precious Miss Templeton that I don't want to see her again. Do you know, she even suggested I went back on the stage?' Her laugh was harsh, brittle. 'I don't want pity—and that's all I'd get if I displayed myself in public!'

Laura bit her lip so hard she drew blood, yet was scarcely aware of the pain. So Helen had been lying after all! What a convincing performance she had put on. Laura had really thought she wanted to be friends, yet listening to the venom in her voice now she knew that it had all been play-acting. That she had despised the thought of Laura seeing her.

She waited breathlessly for Brad's reply, but it was soft and inaudible, so Laura chose that moment to knock, not wishing to be caught eavesdropping. How true it was that a listener never hears any good of oneself, she thought as she opened the door.

Her employer had his back to her, looking ostensibly through the uncurtained window at the star-spangled sky. Helen was in a chair beside him, but she too avoided looking at Laura, examining her impeccably manicured nails as though they were of the utmost importance.

Laura stood awkwardly in the centre of the room wondering why she had been summoned, and wishing one of them would speak instead of ignoring her as though she were an intruder.

At length Brad turned. He looked from Laura to Helen, his eyes softening slightly as they rested on the shining curls. Helen was too intent scrutinising her hands to notice the look he gave her.

'I went to see a specialist while I was away.' His voice was gently persuasive. 'He thinks he may be able to do something for you.'

Helen's head shot up, her eyes ablaze. 'I've had enough of doctors and hospitals! Why on earth do you have to interfere? I won't have anyone else look at me as though I were some prize specimen in a zoo!'

He dropped to his knees beside her. 'Look, Helen,' he cajoled. 'He's very good, the best in his field. He has a private clinic in London. You'll have your own room. It will practically be like living at home.'

'No, I refuse! I don't care how good he is, I'm not going!' Her face was contorted with fury and she banged her fists against Brad's chest.

He caught her hands, trying to still her rage, but Helen snatched free and this time her wrath was directed at Laura. She pointed a red-tipped finger. 'And why did you insist upon *her* being present when you told me?'

Laura too was mystified. The whole conversation was personal. She could not imagine why he had sent for her.

'I had my reasons,' said Brad, 'but if you turn down my suggestion there's no point in discussing the matter any more.' He looked across at his secretary. 'I'm sorry to have dragged you up here for nothing.'

Helen's attitude completely stunned Laura. She could not believe that this was the same charming, friendly person, but as she turned to go Helen's voice halted her.

'Wait. Now you've gone this far, Brad, you may as well tell us how Laura fits into the picture.' Her expression suggested that she thought little of the idea of involving the other girl.

Brad's tones were low but firm. 'No. I was wrong to want to discuss this matter without having told you first.' His eyes were troubled as he looked at Laura. 'If you wouldn't mind?'

'Of course.' Laura closed the door gently, deeply disturbed by the scene that had taken place. It was incredible that Helen should have such an unpleasant side to her nature, or was that the true person, and the delightful girl of yesterday a front for her benefit? Slowly she went downstairs, confused and unable to decide which was the real person. It must be a family trait, she said to herself ironically, for both Brad and his sister to have dual personalities.

Back in the lounge she no longer felt like knitting. Helen's reaction worried her. Surely the possibility of a cure should produce excitement? Anything would be better than the prospect of spending the rest of her life as an invalid. It was unbelievable that she should flatly reject Brad's offer after all the trouble he had taken. He looked so worried when asking her to leave. If only there was something she could do. But what? It was obvious Helen would not listen to any pleas Laura made on Brad's behalf. It was up to Brad himself to persuade his sister.

The logs glowed red and as Laura stared thoughtfully at the ever-changing pattern she did not hear the door quietly open, or footsteps cross the room.

She jumped as Brad's voice broke into her thoughts. 'So there you are. I've been looking for you.'

He sank wearily on to the companion armchair at the

other side of the fireplace. Tired lines etched round his eyes and mouth made Laura want to comfort him. She forgot the row they had had earlier, forgot the way he treated her when something went wrong with his work. He was a tired, worried man and needed a woman's care.

All at once he smiled, his face clearing miraculously. 'I think I've persuaded her,' he said, his voice low and vibrant. 'At least, she's promised to think it over, and knowing Helen that's as good as saying yes.'

'I'm so pleased. Do you really think that this specialist will cure her?' Laura's eagerness brought a glow to her eyes. It would be wonderful if Helen could walk again. There would be no more bitterness, she could take up her life as an actress and Brad would be relieved of the responsibility of looking after her—a burden he would be more than pleased to relinquish, if Helen was to be believed. The trouble was, Laura was not now sure which was truth and which had been a story conjured up by Helen for her benefit.

'I've every confidence in Doctor Jorgensen. If he can't help, no one can. God knows she's seen enough doctors. But this one's top-notch. I'm sorry to have involved you in that scene just now. I didn't know she'd react like that. I thought that perhaps your presence would help, but I was wrong.'

She made an involuntary gesture towards him. 'Don't worry. So long as she's agreed that's all that matters.'

He nodded his thanks and selected a cigar from a box on a marble-topped low table. Laura watched as he lighted it, the smoke spiralling upwards. His square brown hands did not look as though they belonged to a writer. They were strong and capable like those of a manual worker. In fact his whole body held a strength, a vitality. He looked in perfect physical condition. It must be all his dashing about, thought Laura inconsequentially, for he didn't take any other form of exercise as far as she knew.

He frowned as he smoked, as though trying to solve a problem. Eventually he spoke. 'Laura, I'm sorry for my behaviour this afternoon. I ought not to have shouted like that.'

His peace-offering moved her deeply. He was a proud man and she knew how much it must have cost him to apologise. 'I, too, was at fault. I should have let you explain—do you think you could tell me now?' She lowered her eyes. 'I couldn't help overhearing you scolding Helen.' Looking from beneath her lashes, she saw the surprise on his face. 'So as it seems I've become unintentionally involved I should like to know more about your sister and why she shuts herself away.'

Brad stood, his back to the fire, looking down into his secretary's troubled face. 'I wish I knew what went on inside that head of hers.' Lips compressed, he turned, flicking his unfinished cigar into the dying embers. 'She's been entirely different since the accident. She used to be so full of fun and life, and now look at her—more bitter every day.' His voice became hard. 'It's all my fault. I did this to her—took away the very life she lived for.'

Laura failed to understand Brad's reasoning—unless there was something she still did not know. She spoke softly, 'How can you be to blame?'

He swung round. 'Didn't she tell you? I was driving at the time of the accident and she doesn't let me forget it. It's her own idea to stay up there. She won't let anyone see her—that's why I was so amazed when I found out that you'd been up. I thought she'd be distraught and that I'd have another of her scenes.'

The anguish in his eyes caused Laura's heart to fill with sympathy. 'I'm sorry. I see now why you reacted so violently, but at the time I honestly thought Helen was telling the truth.'

'And condemned me straight away?'

Laura looked at him sharply, but he was smiling.

'Well—yes, but I had no reason to disbelieve Helen. If only you'd told me! David said you lived with your sister and I was puzzled when no mention was made of her.'

His lips curved humorously. 'Our first meeting hardly rated confidences. I hope that will all be changed now.'

Laura, who had been watching a shower of sparks shoot up the chimney as one of the remaining logs changed its position, raised her head at the unusual warmth in his voice, but his face belied little of his feelings.

Clasping his hands behind his back, Brad walked across to the window, turning there to look directly at Laura. 'When Helen goes to London I want you to go with her.' He paused a moment, watching the effect his request had on Laura. 'I have a flat there which you can use. She'll need someone close at hand.'

Surprised that Brad should even contemplate her accompanying his sister after the way Helen had spoken, Laura cried, 'Oh, no, Brad, it wouldn't work. I did once feel that Helen and I might be friends, but after hearing her ... And what about your typing?'

'To hell with my work. Helen's future's more important at the moment. You don't know how it grieves me to have her sit up there day after day, knowing it's my fault. I never thought she was the type to do a thing like this. When we were children one of our friends was an invalid and Helen was always the first to talk to him.

The other children made fun, but never Helen.'

'Don't you see,' said Laura, 'that's probably why she acts like this. She's afraid people will make fun of her as they did that child.'

'Mmm.' He returned to his chair. 'You could be right, but I don't think her friends would treat her like that. It's only when we're children that we're cruel.'

'True, but obviously Helen has a fixation about being made fun of—or pitied—which is just as bad. I hope this doctor can help.'

'You can say that again. It would be the end as far as Helen's concerned if she allowed herself to be subjected to further treatment only to find it all in vain. She's suffered enough these last twelve months.' His eyes met and pleaded with hers. 'You will go? It's no good me going—she resents me far too much. Have a word with her now. I'm sure she didn't mean half the things she said.'

'If you really think—? She *was* quite friendly towards me in the beginning, so perhaps—'

Laura was doubtful whether Helen would appreciate her interfering, but if Brad wished it, she was employed to do as he asked. He had made that clear from the beginning.

They rose together. Laura, forgetting the bag of knitting at the side of her chair, caught her foot in the handle and stumbled. Immediately Brad sprang forward, his arms protectively around her. At his touch every fibre of her being seemed to be on fire and as she lifted her head to thank him his lips came down on hers. For a second she gave herself up to the thrill of his kiss, then remembrance of the other girls who had fallen for his charm came flooding back. With heightened colour she pushed herself away. She had no desire to be classed in

63

the same category. Shooting him an indignant glance, she rushed from the room.

At the foot of the stairs she paused. His embrace had disturbed her more than she cared to admit. Was she falling in love with this temperamental man? There were times when she hated the sight of him, yet others when—? Perhaps it was compassion she felt, compassion for the sadness and regret he showed over his sister's behaviour? No one likes to see a man so disturbed, least of all a man of Brad's disposition.

'I'm sorry, I shouldn't have done that.'

Laura felt Brad's hand, warm and slightly unsteady, on her shoulder and knew she daren't turn to face him. It must surely be reflected in her face that she had enjoyed his kiss, that the touch of his lips had awoken an undreamed-of response. She closed her eyes, willing herself to shut out the memory of his compelling dark eyes; the hard strength of his body against hers.

'It—it's all right, Brad. Let's forget it.' Without a backward glance she climbed the stairs, fully aware that he watched until she disappeared from his view.

Outside Helen's door she waited until the strength returned to her limbs, the irrational thudding of her heart subsided. She had no desire to explain to Helen the reason for her breathlessness or increased colour.

The reply to her knock was clear and loud, and as Laura entered she was relieved to see Helen's friendly smile. Whatever Brad had said it was plain that she had overcome her antipathy.

Laura sat on the edge of the bed looking across at the other girl. Helen's breathtaking loveliness struck her anew as the light from the crystal chandelier enhanced her perfect bone structure and faultless complexion. It was truly sad, she thought, that the world should be deprived of so beautiful an actress, and she fervently hoped that this further treatment would be a success.

'Brad tells me that you've agreed to see this specialist, Helen. I'm so glad. I'm sure you're doing the right thing.'

Helen's smile faded. 'Are you? I wish I had your confidence. I swore after the last time that I'd never see another doctor, but Brad assures me that this one's different.'

'Then I'm sure he must be. Helen—' Laura hesitated, not sure how to phrase her next sentence, 'I'm sorry if I upset you this morning. I didn't mean to. I had no idea how you felt.'

'Brad's been talking about me?' Helen's lips curled in contempt. 'What else has he told you that you didn't already know?'

'You're wrong, Helen. Brad hasn't said anything at all except how guilty he feels. You see, I accidentally overheard him telling you off when I came up earlier.'

'So he's arranged this specialist to appease his own conscience? Not because he's concerned about me?' She pouted, spoiling for a moment her well shaped lips.

'Of course not,' indignantly. 'Brad thinks the world of you. He wants to help. It's sheer bad luck the accident happened while he was driving, but you can't blame him for it. It could have been anyone. Forget what happened. Concentrate on getting better—you do want to walk again?'

'What do *you* think? I don't enjoy living in this dead-and-alive hole. I'd give anything to get back to my old life, my old friends—if they haven't forgotten me.' Longing combined with discontent in these last words revealing an inner torture. Laura could not help feeling sorry for the other girl even though she now knew that it was Helen's own fault her friends had deserted her. She had no one to blame but herself for her present boredom and loneliness.

'How would you like it if I came with you to London?' asked Laura lightly. 'Then I could see you every day. There's nothing worse than being in a strange place on your own. I've learned that from bitter experience.'

'Would you?' Helen's voice rose hopefully, then dropped. 'But Brad—he'd never let you. He thinks more of his work than me.'

'Brad's already asked, so you have nothing to worry about.' Laura rose and dropped a kiss on Helen's cheek. 'Everything's going to be all right, you'll see. Goodnight.'

Not wishing to run the risk of bumping into Brad again, Laura went straight to her own room. Without switching on the light she crossed to the window and stared out at the luminous moon which enhanced the countryside in its silvery beam. It looked so inviting that impulsively she slipped a coat round her shoulders and quietly let herself out of the house.

The air was cold, but Laura welcomed its freshness against her hot cheeks. The memory of Brad's kiss was uppermost in her mind and she could not help wondering what had motivated him. Was it because he wanted to kiss her or was it an impulsive reaction caused by their being thrust together? She did not think he was a man usually given to impulses, but on the other hand he had never given her any reason to believe that he held any affection for her. Apart from the two occasions they had met in Shrewsbury he had had scant regard for her feelings, in fact he seemed to enjoy humiliating her whenever possible.

The shrill hoot of an owl startled Laura. She had wandered farther than she intended. The house was now out of sight and heavy moisture in the grass and leaves beneath the trees soon soaked through her shoes. She shivered, pulling her thin coat more closely. Retracing her steps, she gently pushed open the heavy door. Not wishing to disturb anyone, she took off her shoes and padded with wet feet across the cold marble floor. She had almost reached the staircase when Brad's study door opened. Caught in the stream of light, Laura looked guiltily over her shoulder.

'Where on earth have you been?' Brad sounded concerned, despite the sharp note in his voice, but as the light behind him threw his face into shadow she was unable to read his expression. Even so she was acutely aware of his tall leanness as he stood silhouetted in the door frame, and wondered whether he too was remembering their earlier embrace. 'And why are you carrying your shoes as though you were an intruder?'

'I—I went for a walk and I didn't want to interrupt you. I thought you might be working and if you heard a noise out here you would—'

He snapped on the hall light, noticing for the first time her soaking feet. 'You silly child, what are you trying to do? Catch pneumonia? Come inside and get off those wet stockings while I heat some milk.'

Obediently Laura entered his study, taking off her tights and curling her toes before the fire. Despite Brad's anger he had been genuinely concerned about her well-being, and the thought brought a comforting warmth not entirely due to the glowing logs.

He returned in a remarkably short time with the drink and a towel. While Laura dried her feet he poured a measure of whisky into the milk.

Laura wrinkled her nose when she saw what he was doing. 'Ugh! I don't like whisky.'

'Like it or not, you're going to drink it,' he said gruffly, standing over her while she forced the burning liquid down her throat. His eyes were unusually kind and Laura's heart beat a tattoo in her breast. She hastily lowered her lashes, puzzled by her own reaction to his solicitude.

When she had finished he took the glass, setting it aside on his desk before pulling her to her feet. 'Come now, straight to bed before you catch cold. I don't want anything to stop you going to London. I've arranged everything for tomorrow, before Helen changes her mind.'

Laura felt rebuffed. So that was the reason for his concern, she thought, as together they climbed the stairs. She had been idiotic enough to believe that his benevolence was for her own sake. When in fact he merely wanted to make sure she was well enough to accompany Helen.

Outside her door he halted. He tipped her chin with his finger and for one moment Laura thought he was going to kiss her again. His eyes smouldered like twin coals and her heart beat so loudly she was sure he must hear it. She waited expectantly, but after giving her a long, searching look as if trying to see into the depths of her mind Brad gave a barely perceptible sigh and pushed his hands into his pockets. 'Good-night, sleep well,' he said, and continued along the corridor to his own room.

Puzzled by his attitude, Laura prepared for bed, but tired as she was she could not sleep. She lay awake watching the patterns cast on the ceiling by the moon as it shone through the branches of the trees.

She ran over in her mind the events of the day—from the thrilling moment when Brad had kissed her to the tenderness he had shown a few minutes earlier. Even though she now knew his concern was not entirely for her own sake, even though she knew she would never be anything more to him than his secretary—hadn't he made that clear by the way he'd apologised for kissing her, by the way he'd shortly said good-night just now when she herself had anticipated another kiss? Despite all this, she came to the startling conclusion that she was in love, completely and irrevocably in love.

'But I can't be,' she whispered aloud, sitting bolt upright. 'How can I fall for such an insufferable person?' Rather than feel comforted by her discovery Laura was tormented by the distressing position in which she now found herself and it was several hours later before she finally fell into a fitful sleep, waking with a start when her alarm told her that it was seven-thirty.

Laura mused for a moment at the warm glow that filled her, then flushed almost guiltily as remembrance of the previous evening returned. Whatever happened she must not let Brad guess at her feelings. She could imagine his amusement. His complacency that she was following the same pattern. Had he kissed any of his other secretaries? she wondered. Had he given them any encouragement? Finding the thought distasteful, she pushed it firmly from her.

She showered and dressed, choosing with care a jade green woollen dress which enhanced the slim perfection of her figure, recalling that today she was leaving for London and realising with something approaching dismay that she did not want to go. Although there was little likelihood of Brad ever returning her love she wanted to be near him, to hear his deep voice, watch the changing emotions cross his rugged face. I don't want to go with Helen, she told herself, mildly angry that this should happen now. I want to stay here with Brad. Then the knowledge of how much his sister's health meant to him came flooding back. By accompanying Helen she would be pleasing Brad, and after all, it would not be for long, a month or two at the most, and surely he would visit them occasionally? Knowing how fond he was of the other girl Laura knew he would not leave them there without frequently checking on Helen's progress.

Entering the dining-room, Laura was surprised to see Brad seated at the table, apparently waiting for her. Her shock must have been apparent, for he laughed. 'I thought I'd give you the pleasure of my company this morning, as it will be the last time you eat here for a while. You don't mind?'

'N-no, of course not. It will make quite a change.' Her heart hammered painfully as she slid into her chair. How handsome he looked this morning, his white, roll-necked shirt causing his tan to appear even darker.

His grey eyes watched her closely. 'No after-effects? You seem a little shaky.'

Thank goodness he'd put down her reaction to the events of the night before, thought Laura. She would have to be more careful in future, or he would soon guess the way she felt. 'No, I'm fine. I didn't sleep too well, that's all.'

Brad passed her the milk, their fingers touching for one electric moment as she took it from him. How true was the saying that hate is akin to love, thought Laura. She had detested Brad intensely at the beginning, and now here she was head over heels in love. If only he felt the same way about her! But she knew how unlikely that was. She was his employee and as such must try and remember her position.

Waiting until she had poured the milk on to her cereal, Brad said, 'I've been walking in the woods this morning. I love autumn, the russets, greens and golds, the rustle of leaves beneath my feet. It's a pity you're leaving. You'll miss the best part of the year.'

'I know. Autumn's always been my favourite. I remember when I was young collecting and pressing as many different coloured leaves as I could find. I treasured them for years.'

Brad smiled. 'Autumn treasure, eh? Your hair's like autumn, you know that? Sometimes it's gold—like now with the sun shining on it, and another time it's pure copper—as that leaf blowing across the lawn. I think I treasure you as you did those leaves—I really don't know what I'd have done without you this last week or two.'

Laura felt her colour rise. If only he knew what his words were doing to her! Managing to return his smile, she said shakily, 'Thank you for the compliment, but I'm sure anyone else could have done just as well.'

'Don't you believe it.' He raised his eyes skyward. 'How I've suffered at the hands of scheming females!'

Feeling more and more uncomfortable by Brad's unaccustomed friendliness, Laura had difficulty in hiding her feelings and was glad when breakfast was over.

'I suggest you go and help Helen pack,' said Brad as they left the dining-room, 'and Laura,' his hand resting lightly on her shoulder, 'I'm glad you're going. She needs someone to stand by her during the next few weeks.'

'Are you coming with us?' asked Laura, her shoulder burning at his touch.

71

'I'm sorry. I can't manage it. My man, Jarvis, will take you down in the Jag. Everything's been arranged.'

Helen was in excellent spirits. Obviously she had now decided that the treatment was going to be a success and couldn't wait to get going. 'It's the first time I've left the house for twelve months,' she said excitedly. 'It will be good to be back in London. Even in the clinic I shall sense the atmosphere—the night life—everything I used to love.'

'I'm glad you feel like this,' replied Laura, snapping the fasteners on Helen's case. 'I was worried that you'd change your mind.'

Helen raised her finely pencilled brows. 'You really are concerned about me, aren't you? It's nice to know that at last someone cares. If you wern't going with me I shouldn't go. I couldn't face it on my own.' She suddenly smiled. 'I like you, Laura. I'm sorry for speaking the way I did yesterday.'

'There's no need to apologise. I should probably feel the same in your circumstances. It's enough to make anyone bitter.—I'll tell Brad you're ready now. We'll soon be on our way.'

Jarvis took them straight to the clinic where Helen was shown to a room which was more like a hotel apartment than a hospital ward. It was thickly carpeted and luxuriously furnished. A supply of books and magazines were beside the bed on one side and a telephone on the other. Helen looked round her with undisguised pleasure. 'Brad's certainly spared no expense. Let's hope this Doctor Jorgensen's as good as he says.'

'And what has Brad Stuart been saying about me?' came a deep voice from behind them.

'Eric!' Helen spun round the chair which had been

used to wheel her into the room, her face contorted in horror. 'Oh, no!' She buried her head in her hands. 'Brad's done this on purpose. He knew very well I didn't want anyone I knew to see me like this.'

Doctor Jorgensen smiled, taking no notice at all of Helen's fury. 'And if I didn't see you, I couldn't cure you. It's as simple as that. You can't really make me believe that you want to spend the rest of your life—' a slight pause and then with deliberate emphasis, 'a cripple!'

If he thought his words would goad Helen into staying he was wrong, for she jerked up her head and with eyes full of hatred said, 'How dare you speak to me like that! Laura, fetch Jarvis. I'm going home. I refuse to let this man treat me. If I'd known it was him I should never have come in the first place.'

Laura looked hesitantly from Helen's enraged face to the calm, smiling doctor. He was a short, stocky man in his mid-thirties and obviously not in the least put out by Helen's reaction 'Wait outside a few minutes, please. I'd like to talk to Helen alone.'

Doubtfully and trying to ignore the agonised look Helen threw her, Laura made her way to the waiting-room a few doors away.

Had Brad been aware that Helen knew Eric Jorgensen? Laura mused. He knew how insistent she was that none of her friends should see her. The name Doctor Jorgensen had apparently meant nothing to Helen until she heard his voice, so perhaps Brad did not know either. It was sheer bad luck that it should turn out like this and Laura fervently hoped that the doctor would be able to persuade Helen to stay. After all the trouble and expense Brad had gone to it would be dreadful if Helen flatly refused to co-operate. Strangely, Doctor Jorgensen had not seemed in the least perturbed by Helen's outburst. Perhaps he had expected something like this and had a plan of action already worked out?

Nervously Laura crossed to the window. She could see Jarvis waiting outside. He must be wondering why she was taking so long. She had told him she would only be a few minutes.

Her name was suddenly called and turning she saw the doctor standing in the doorway, the same lopsided smile still on his lips. 'She'll be all right now. I'm sorry it happened like that. Her brother warned me that she refused to see anyone connected with her past, so I didn't tell him I'd met Helen. Otherwise I knew she wouldn't come, and I'm confident that I shall be able to cure her.'

'But why didn't she know when Brad mentioned your name?'

'We'd only met socially and she knew me as Eric. She didn't even know I was a doctor. Anyway, I think I've convinced her now that I can help, so if you'd like to go in—'

He stood back, allowing Laura to precede him. As they entered Helen smiled up from the depths of the armchair on which she now sat. Laura breathed a sigh of relief. It looked as though everything was going to work out after all.

CHAPTER FIVE

THE telephone rang as Laura re-entered the flat. Brad's voice sounded warm and friendly. 'I wanted to make sure that Helen's settled in all right, and you, of course. How do you like my flat?'

'It—it's fine—but I never imagined you to have a place like this.' Laura looked round at the streamlined furniture, the brightly painted walls and boldly designed carpet.

A chuckle reached her. 'You're right—it isn't me. But I rent it furnished and for the little time I spend there I've managed to shut my eyes to the decor. It serves its purpose—that's all I can say for it.' His voice became serious. 'How's Helen?'

'Okay now, but I thought for a time that we'd have to bring her home.'

Laura heard his quick intake of breath. 'Why? What happened?'

'She knows Doctor Jorgensen.'

'Oh no! Of all things I never suspected that—her crowd were all theatricals. How did he come to meet him?'

'At some party or other. They weren't close friends by any means, but sufficiently friendly for her to refuse to let him have anything to do with her.'

'What happened next?'

She could sense Brad's anxiety and hastened to re-assure him. 'Doctor Jorgensen's charm worked wonders. He made her realise how silly she was and how unfair

75

she was being to you—'

He snorted. 'I bet that did some good.'

'No, you're wrong. I don't know exactly what the doctor said, but her hostilities are down and she seems perfectly happy. Jarvis brought my luggage here, then I went back and spent the whole evening with her. She's different already, Brad, quite gay and talking about going back on the stage.'

'Let's hope our faith is justified,' Brad said grimly. 'I hope he hasn't given her false hopes.'

'I shouldn't think so. It's more than he would dare do.'

'I shan't feel happy until I actually see her walking again. If anything goes wrong she'll blame me more than ever.'

'Brad!' Laura pleaded. 'You're not to think like that. You've done what you thought was the right thing and now we must wait.'

'I wish I was with you, but it's impossible. I'll try and get down in a few days. Keep me informed of any developments.'

A warm glow enveloped Laura as she replaced the receiver. Hearing his voice had re-awoken the feelings she was trying so hard to forget. At the stormy beginning of their relationship love had been the furthest thought from her mind. She had felt he wasn't her type at all, yet here she was—completely under his spell. And there was nothing she could do about it.

Laura spent most of her time with Helen during the following days and the two girls became firm friends. There were occasions when Helen complained that they did not seem to be doing anything towards making her better, but Laura reasonably pointed out that they had to observe her case in the first place and that she must be patient. What were a few days or weeks compared to a lifetime of inactivity?

And then for two days running Laura was not allowed at the clinic as Doctor Jorgenson wished to carry out some extensive tests. Time passed very slowly and Laura felt more lonely than ever before. If only Brad could spare the time to visit them—but she knew that was impossible. He had telephoned her the evening before saying how snowed under with work he was and it would be a good job when she was back. He hadn't realised exactly how much work she had taken off his hands. Laura suggested he bring some of it to the flat, but he refused, insisting she enjoy her break.

On the second day of her 'holiday' Laura browsed round the shops, admiring the Christmas displays which already added a festive air to the scene. She was walking slowly along Oxford Street deliberating whether to return to the flat or make her way to Hyde Park and enjoy a breath of fresh air when a heavy hand clapped her on the shoulder.

'Laura Templeton! What on earth are you doing here at this time of day? Shouldn't you be tapping away at your typewriter?'

'Mr. Harvey!' Laura smiled warmly at the young man in the expensive suit and flashy tie. 'How nice to see someone I know.'

'Philip, please.' He swung into stride beside her. 'But you haven't answered my question. Don't say Mr. Greg's given you the sack? You were looking very despondent just now.'

'He's emigrated—didn't you know? Although I suppose you wouldn't unless you had any further business with him.'

He shook his long fair hair, his dazzling smile revealing even white teeth. 'I'd no idea.' He caught her hand. 'Come and have coffee and tell me what you're doing with yourself these days. I couldn't believe my luck when I saw you here.'

Laura allowed herself to be led into a nearby restaurant and when they were settled told him about her new job and the reason she was in London.

'So—you're alone,' when she had finished. 'Must do something about that. How about dinner this evening?'

Too late Laura realised that her enthusiasm at meeting a familiar face had given Philip the wrong impression. He was not her sort at all. With plenty of money in his pocket he was out for a good time. 'I'm sorry, but I'm expecting my employer to ring at nine. He likes to know how Helen's progressing.'

'That's all right.' Philip brushed away her excuse. 'I'll pick you up at quarter past. We'll wine and dine and I'll show you a side of London you've never seen before.'

His manner was so persuasive that Laura found herself agreeing. One date won't hurt, she decided. The change would do her good.

Fortunately she had brought a long dress with her, packed on the spur of the moment in case Brad turned up and asked her out for an evening, and as she showered and dressed she began to look forward to Philip's company. Despite his too-familiar attitude he was good fun and the diversion was just what she needed.

When the bell rang, Laura slipped a wrap round her shoulders and opened the door. Philip's dazzling smile faded when he realised she was not going to ask him in, but he quickly regained his composure and escorted her out to his waiting Triumph.

'You look very beautiful, Laura. You should always wear your hair loose.'

'Thank you,' replied Laura primly, 'but it's not very practical when I'm working.'

The car slid smoothly away and Laura found it pleasant to be in the company of a man who made no pretence of the fact that he found her attractive, even though she would have much preferred her escort to be Brad.

'I'm taking you to a nightclub I know.' He slanted her a glance. 'The world's your oyster tonight.'

For the first time Laura experienced a feeling of apprehension. Had she been wise in accepting Philip's invitation? Had she let herself in for more than she had bargained? Firmly she pushed these doubts to the back of her mind. If Philip Harvey started any funny business she was quite capable of dealing with him. He would not be the first man to make unwanted passes. She had had enough of that sort of thing when working for David. A girl alone was a target for such men, especially as the business had not boasted a waiting-room and any visitors had had to sit in her office. Philip had been a typical example and she realised now that she should not have been so friendly when they met earlier. He would certainly take it the wrong way.

'I didn't realise we were going anywhere like that. I thought a hotel or restaurant—but a nightclub—I've never been to one before.'

'Then now's the time to find out, my sweet.' His hand left the steering wheel and rested for a moment on hers. 'You don't know what you've been missing.'

Laura pulled away sharply. 'I'm not sure that I've been missing anything. That side of life doesn't appeal to me.'

'Come now, honey. Surely every woman dreams of glamour and riches?'

'Maybe the women in your life do, but not this one. I'm a country girl at heart. Why do you think I took that job in Shropshire?'

'I've no idea. But you can't fool me that you weren't feeling lonely when I saw you this afternoon?'

'Maybe I was, but it doesn't mean I want to spend all my time searching for excitement.' She sensed Philip's withdrawal and immediately regretted her sharp words. 'Don't get me wrong—I'm looking forward to my evening out. I just don't want you to get the wrong impression.'

He flashed her a smile. 'That's my girl! I knew I hadn't underestimated you.' As the car glided to a halt outside the large, impressive building, Laura swallowed her apprehension, preparing to enjoy herself. Their table was set back in a tiny alcove, yet still permitted full view of the stage where an attractive girl was singing a current pop song. As they ordered their meal Laura realised that Philip must be a regular customer. He only had to raise his hand and a waiter appeared. It was amazing what money could do, she thought, although it was very pleasant to receive such deferential treatment.

They ate their meal in silence, enjoying the antics of a comedian who had followed the girl. Once or twice Laura felt Philip looking at her with more than a hint of admiration in his blue eyes, but she resolutely ignored his overtures and concentrated on the excellent duck with orange sauce which was the speciality of the evening.

When Philip ordered her a brandy she was about to protest, as she was already feeling the effects of the dinner wine. but realising that he would be offended by her refusal, she took a steady sip, determined to make it last her all evening. She was not accustomed to drink and didn't want to disgrace herself in front of Philip.

A group of musicians appeared on the stage and several couples whirled round the limited space of the dance area. Philip took Laura's hand as the music changed to a dreamy waltz. 'Come, my sweet. I'm sure you dance as divinely as you look.'

After a few circles of the floor, Philip's arm tightened round Laura's back. 'You're the most beautiful woman in the room,' he whispered. 'We must do this more often.'

Laura stiffened and tried to pull back her head, but short of creating a scene she was forced to stay within the confines of his arms. 'Do you say that to all the girls?' she asked stiffly, 'or am I being singled out for special treaatment? If so I'm afraid you're wasting your time.'

'What do you mean, sweetheart? Aren't you enjoying yourself?' The shock on Philip's face made Laura want to laugh. He didn't look as though he was used to such replies.

'Of course I am. Who wouldn't, with such superb food and a handsome escort? But don't get carried away. This is a one-time date and don't you forget it.'

'Laura!' His arms relaxed their hold and his expression became all at once serious. 'You don't really mean that? I wanted to ask you out when you worked for David Greg, but he always seemed to keep his beady eye on you. But there's nothing to stop you seeing me now?' He looked at her left hand. 'You're not engaged or anything?'

'Er—no. But I'm in London on business, not pleasure.'

'You can't be on duty all the while. You must have some spare time.' He pulled her close again. 'Anyway, let's not spoil the evening. I'm sure you'll change your mind before the night's over.'

The dancing finished and they returned to their table, Laura thankful to be free from Philip's all too passionate caresses. He was proving more of a handful than she had at first thought and she took a long sip of brandy to steady her ruffled nerves.

Later, when the cabaret finished, Philip suggested they go and play the gaming tables in the room below, but Laura refused. The idea of gambling was distasteful to her, but rather than admit this she insisted that she was tired. 'I've had such a full day that I really must get to bed. I want to be at the clinic early in the morning.'

Surprisingly he did not argue and had the car waiting outside when Laura emerged from fetching her wrap. He was unusually silent during the journey and Laura, who really did feel tired now, did not attempt to make any conversation.

On arrival he switched off the engine and caught her hands in his. 'Sweetheart, you will come out with me again? You didn't mean what you said earlier?'

He looked so pathetic that Laura felt a pang of remorse, but she was determined not to let the friendship develop. It was no use encouraging him when she knew nothing could arise from their relationship. Her heart belonged to Brad, even though he was aware of the remoteness of his ever returning her love.

'I'm sorry, Philip. I did mean it. Thank you for a most enjoyable evening.' She kissed him lightly on the cheek and slid from the car before he had time to realise what she was doing.

Once in the flat she took off her dress, hanging it carefully in the wardrobe before slipping into a blue nylon housecoat. She made herself a cup of coffee and curled up on the settee. Philip's demanding company had taken more out of her than she thought. She felt drained of all energy. He was thoughtful and charming, she could not deny that, but his idea of a good time was not hers. Although—if Brad had taken her out for such an evening would she be feeling the same as she did now? In all honesty she knew the answer was no. Wherever she went with Brad—whether it was a simple walk in the country or dining out at the most expensive restaurant—she knew without a doubt it would be enjoyable. If only he wasn't so arrogantly superior! She sighed. It was no use wishing for the moon. To Brad she was his secretary and that was all there was to it. Even if he had kissed her she could only put it down to an impulsive action that he immediately regretted.

As for Philip, it was a pity she could not return his feelings, for he was good company, except that she wouldn't mind betting he treated all his women the same. Look how the staff at the Golden Crest had jumped to his attention. He must be a very good customer indeed and she couldn't see him tying himself down to one girl. She was glad she hadn't given him any encouragement. He was the type to want all the advantages of marriage without the formalities that went with it.

Helen was sitting up in bed when Laura arrived the next morning, a frothy creation of blue lace draped casually round her shoulders. Her face lit up at the sight of her friend. 'Am I glad to see you? It's been a long two days and I'm absolutely worn out with all the examinations. But guess what?' Her eyes shone with excitement. 'Eric says he's confident he can cure me!'

Laura sat on the edge of the bed and hugged Helen, tears of happiness stinging the back of her eyes. 'What wonderful news! Brad will be delighted.'

Helen closed her eyes. 'Doesn't it sound marvellous? I never thought it would be possible. Oh, Laura, if it really happens I shall never forgive myself for treating Brad the way I have. He must think me the rottenest sister any man can have.'

'Of course he doesn't. What you've been through was bound to make you feel disgruntled—he said so himself.'

'You sound as though you're championing him.' Helen smiled slowly. 'Don't tell me you've fallen for him as well?'

Laura felt the tell-tale colour creep into her cheeks and quickly turned away, taking off her coat and hanging it on a hook behind the door. 'That's hardly likely, the way he treats me,' she said over her shoulder. 'I've never met a more tyrannical person.'

Helen laughed. 'You get used to that—it's just his way.'

Sinking on to a chair at the side of the bed, Laura smiled wryly. 'I could imagine what would happen if I ignored his commands. I'd be out of a job in double quick time.'

'I'm not so sure. He won't get another secretary like you very easily. I bet if you tried you could twist him round your little finger. Don't you fancy him one little bit?'

Laura pretended to consider the question. 'Well—he is handsome, and can be quite nice if he tries, but I'm afraid we never see eye to eye.'

'I doubt if you will,' returned Helen. 'You're too much alike—in temperament, I mean,' she added in reply to Laura's frown.

'Heaven forbid that I should ever be classed with him!' laughed Laura. 'Am I really?'

'No. You're far too nice a person to suffer with Brad's bad habits.' Her face became all at once serious. 'I'm awfully glad you came to us, Laura. Otherwise I'd never have come here. Brad probably knew that and used you as an ally.'

'An ally?' Laura raised her brows. 'He practically told me it was my duty to come.'

'Yes, but he hadn't planned it that way. Remember the day he asked me, when he insisted you be present? Well, he thought I wouldn't refuse him in front of you and hoped I'd be the one to suggest you accompany me. He hadn't reckoned on my temper and the plan misfired.'

'I see,' said Laura. 'I've often wondered exactly why he asked me up there. I suppose you'll desert Leastone Hall once you're on your feet again—return to your beloved theatre?'

'Naturally. It's my whole life—at least it was, and with a bit of luck it will be again.' She crossed her fingers. 'Here's hoping!'

Laura thought what a difference there was in this laughing, happy girl from the petulant discontented person she had heard complaining, and was glad that Brad had arranged for her to come with Helen. She did not doubt for a moment the truth in Helen's words that she would not have come had it not been for herself, and now there seemed every possibility that the treatment would be a success. Please God, let it be, she silently prayed. Otherwise who knows what it will do to Helen.

'Tell me what you've been doing with yourself for the last two days,' said Helen, sliding down in bed and regarding Laura artfully. 'Looking up old boy-friends?'

'Nothing so exciting. I spent Monday cleaning the flat and yesterday I went shopping. I did bump into an old acquaintance, though, and he took me out for dinner last night—you needn't look like that, Helen. There's nothing between us. He's definitely not my type, although I imagine you would find him fun.'

'Tell me more,' breathed Helen dramatically.

'Well—he's fairly tall, slim, reasonably good-looking and has a great personality. He has longish blond hair, dresses smartly if a bit way-out. He has plenty of money —rich parents, I suppose.'

'Sounds dishy. Where did you meet him?' asked Helen dreamily.

'He was a customer of David's. Says he always wanted to ask me for a date in those days but hadn't the nerve. Not that I believe him—I think he fancies himself as something of a Don Juan.'

'When are you seeing him again?'

'I'm not,' was Laura's emphatic reply. 'He wouldn't need much encouragement, that one, and I don't intend getting involved.'

'Pity. I'd like to meet him when I'm better.' Then in sudden horror, 'You didn't tell him about me?'

'Well, yes. But why? It's no secret.'

'You don't know how much I hate being unable to walk.' Helen's voice shook vehemently. 'I had enough pity at the time of the accident—that's why I shut myself away and vowed I'd never see anyone else.'

'Dear Helen!' Laura pulled her chair closer. 'We'll never see eye to eye over this. It's inevitable people will

86

commiserate with you at first—I did myself, but they would soon forget your disability, if you'd let them. You're such a wonderful person—when you're not feeling sorry for yourself. I'm sure if Philip ever met you he'd be so bowled over by your looks that nothing else would matter.'

'You think so?' Helen unconsciously patted her hair into place, a pleased smile curving her lips.

'I'm sure. But I don't know why we're talking like this. It's doubtful I'll see him again.'

Helen pouted prettily. 'I hope you do. Then when— if I get better and Brad comes down we could make a foursome. It would be terrific.'

Brad telephoned the clinic later in the day and hearing Helen's excited conversation Laura could imagine his pleasure, his relief that the outcome of this course of treatment was likely to be a success. In her mind's eye she could picture the sudden darkening of his eyes, the way they crinkled at the corners when he was in a good humour, the curve of his lips which completely altered his arrogant features.

She wished she could speak to him, listen to the deep, well-modulated tones of his voice, but this was not to be, and when Helen replaced the receiver she felt a pang of disappointment that he had not even asked after her. Why, oh, why did she have to fall in love with such an impossible man who had not the slightest interest in her? Had he ever been in love? she mused. Did he know what it was like to eat one's heart out for the unattainable? She doubted it. His confident self-assurance was impregnable. The woman to penetrate the chink in his armour would have to be someone pretty special.

Realising that Helen was speaking, Laura dragged

herself away from her thoughts.

'Brad's awfully pleased. He said he might be able to get down tomorrow. He has to see his publisher or something. I bet that's why he rang—to see what sort of reception he'd get from me. Otherwise he would have turned up out of the blue. Anyway, I've forgiven him now, thanks to you—you've made me aware of how idiotically I've behaved and even if things don't go as planned—well—' she shrugged lightly, 'I'll know it's not because Brad doesn't care. No one could do more for me than he has—only I've been too stupid to realise it. I was so bigoted, felt so sorry for myself, that I had no feeling for those around me. I'd no idea I was making other people's lives a misery.'

'I knew you'd come to your senses sooner or later,' said Laura softly. 'You couldn't go on like that for ever.'

'Now you're being nice to me, but I suppose it's true—even if I didn't think so at the time.' She stretched her arms delicately above her head and yawned. 'I'm tired, Laura, after all those strenuous tests. Would you mind if I asked you to go?'

Laura rose instantly. 'Of course not. I should have noticed.' She shrugged into her coat and after promising to come the following day left the clinic.

Normally she caught a bus, but as it was a fine day she decided to walk. Over and over in her mind as she walked came the words, 'Brad is coming tomorrow'. Even in the flat, as she cooked her evening meal, she found it impossible to banish her employer from her mind. He filled her every thought. The situation was becoming ridiculous, she decided, as she ate her omelette. She must find something to occupy her mind.

She was washing the dishes when the doorbell rang.

Immediately she thought that Brad had arrived a day early. Hastily drying her hands and with her heart thudding so loudly it seemed to fill the tiny entrance hall, she took a quick glance in the mirror, patted her hair into place, then opened the door.

'Philip!' Her ready smile vanished and her mouth fell open. 'What on earth are you doing here?'

'That's a fine way to greet a friend.' His cheerful grin slipped, but only for a moment. He brought his hands from behind his back, made an exaggerated bow and presented her with a sheath of roses. 'For you, my sweet.'

Oh dear, thought Laura, dismayed. I hope he isn't going to be a nuisance. To hide her confusion she lifted the tightly curled buds to her face, inhaling appreciatively their delicate perfume.

'They're lovely—but you really shouldn't. You know I didn't want to see you again.'

'Y-yes, but you haven't given me a chance.' He moved a step nearer, as if to enter the flat, but Laura firmly kept her hand on the door, effectively blocking the opening. Short of pushing her away he would have to remain outside, but she had reckoned without his persuasive powers.

'Come on, sweetheart. Aren't you going to ask me in? I promise to behave—Scout's honour.' He saluted and looked at her so pleadingly that Laura was forced to laugh.

'You win. But only for a few minutes. I want to wash my hair.' She returned to the kitchen and filling a vase with water carefully arranged the flowers.

'May I help myself to a drink?' Philip called from the lounge.

'I suppose so. Only it doesn't belong to me. This is

my employer's flat.' She entered the room in time to see the knowing look on his face.

'I see. Like that, is it?'

'How dare you?' snapped Laura in a sudden spurt of anger. Why was it that men always misconstrued a situation? 'There's nothing between us at all. In fact he hasn't been here while I've used it. He's not that type.'

'Come off it! No man would miss an opportunity like this—'

'Philip Harvey,' she spat, green eyes flashing, 'if that's what you think you can get out—now!' She stormed past ready to open the door, but he caught her arm, twisting her round to face him.

'Laura, please, let's not quarrel. Perhaps I shouldn't have said that, but what did you expect me to think? Let's have that drink. Surely he won't begrudge us one?' He crossed to the drinks cabinet with easy familiarity as though he owned the place, and Laura felt herself resenting his presence even more.

'What's yours?'

'A small sherry, please.' Her voice was thin and tight and he threw her an imploring glance.

'Look, I'm sorry. Is that what you want? Now, let's be friends.'

He poured himself a large whisky, handing Laura her sherry before sitting lazily on the scarlet leather settee. 'Come and sit here,' patting the seat beside him. 'Or haven't you forgiven me yet?'

'I'm not sure,' replied Laura coolly, ignoring his request and perching on the tubular arm of an easy chair. 'I don't find quips like that easy to forgive.'

'Well, what else do you expect me to do? Get down on my knees?' He saw the flickering of a smile on

Laura's face at his unusual concern and pressed home his advantage. 'I'll even do that if it will help. Such harsh treatment is breaking my heart.' He placed a hand against his chest in such a theatrical gesture that Laura could not help responding.

'You're irrepressible, Philip!' and she burst out laughing.

Consequently they did not hear the door open and it was like this that Brad Stuart found them.

'Just how long has this been going on, Miss Templeton?' Biting tones, and she smarted under them, her colour heightening.

'I don't know what you mean,' she said, standing to face him and trying to control the tremor in her voice. 'Surely I—'

'Don't be stupid,' he cut in shortly. 'Of course you know what I mean. If I had any idea that you intended entertaining your—your men friends in my flat,' with a derisive look at Philip, 'I'd never have asked you to come.'

How dared he speak to her like that! fumed Laura. What right had he to say what she should do in her spare time, or wasn't she supposed to have any? Perhaps he expected her to be with Helen twenty-four hours a day?

'Really, Mr. Stuart,' she got out at last. 'I think you should get your facts right before making such accusations,' her tone as hostile as Brad's. 'This gentleman is a friend of mine and contrary to whatever you may be thinking it's the first time that he or anyone else has been inside this flat.'

His dark eyebrows rose imperceptibly. 'That is quite beside the point. While you're living here I should like to make it clear that I do not wish you to use it as a rendezvous for your boy-friends.'

He threw a further scornful look at Philip, who was still nonchalantly sipping his whisky, looking from one to the other as if wondering what all the fuss was about.

If only he knew how near she had come to throwing Philip out, raged Laura; how little she desired his company. But spurred to greater anger by his unreasonable attitude and without stopping to think of the consequence of her action, she crossed to Philip's side, putting her arm through his.

'Surely you wouldn't expect me to keep him waiting on the doorstep while I got ready?' Her voice was deliberately honey-sweet. 'Not after he's brought me those beautiful roses?'

Brad looked swiftly from Laura to the vase standing on the table, a muscle jerked in his jaw, his eyes darkened and he took a step forward. For a moment Laura thought he intended striking her, then abruptly he turned, pausing in the doorway to cast one further scornful glance at the occupants of the room.

'I hope you enjoy your evening out,' his voice heavily veiled with sarcasm. 'I'll see you in the morning, Miss Templeton.'

The door banged behind him, cutting into the silence like a gun shot. Laura wanted to run after him, beg him not to go, tell him he was making a mistake and that there was nothing between her and Philip. But of course she couldn't. He had doubted her integrity from the beginning, practically accusing her of having an affair with David, and now he's made it clear that he thought she and Philip were ... Oh, what did it matter? He'd never think of her as anything other than an employee—a not very reliable one at that. Why she had to fall in love with such an irritating man, she would never know. But love was like that. It came along un-bidden, insidiously creeping into your heart, and there was nothing you could do about it.

'Laura!'

'I'm sorry.' She was so wrapped in her thoughts she had forgotten about Philip sitting silently at her side.

'Is he always like that? Domineering, I mean. Telling you what to do in your free time.'

'W-ell, it is *his* flat, but he's not usually quite so much the ironmaster, even if he can be a little overbearing.'

'To put it mildly! If he spoke to me like that I'd soon tell him what to do with his job.'

Not if you loved him, said Laura to herself. Not if the mere thought of his presence caused your pulses to race. The rare moments when he had become human, treated her as a friend—an equal, more than compensated for his outbursts of anger.

She moved to the table, absently touching the delicate blooms. 'I happen to like the job, Philip, and don't for-get—if I walked out on him I'd be walking out of a home as well.'

He followed and stood behind her, so near that she could feel the warmth of his breath on the back of her neck. 'There's always my place, sweetheart. You can move in with me any time you like.'

His hands were on her shoulders and anticipating his next move Laura swiftly twisted away. 'How very kind of you. I must remember that.'

He smiled hopefully, missing the heavy sarcasm which accompanied her words. 'You'd find it very comfortable and it wouldn't cost you a penny.'

Not in hard cash, she supposed, but it didn't take much guessing to know what he would expect. 'Thanks for the offer, Philip, and now, if you don't mind, I really must wash my hair.'

His lips twisted wryly. 'I thought it too good to be true when you told your boss that you were coming out with me. Sure you won't change your mind? He might come back.'

'I doubt it,' she said shortly, and as Philip still made no effort to move she led the way into the hall and opened the door. 'Good-night, Philip.'

'Being thrown out, am I?' but his words were light and as he walked past his lips brushed her cheek in a friendly gesture which Laura imagined was not his usual way of doing things.

She leaned back against the door, conscious of the relief that his departure gave. Aware too of the fact that had he not been present when Brad arrived the evening might have turned out very differently.

It was with mixed feelings that she eventually made her way to bed. What on earth had made her give Brad the impression that Philip meant something to her?

Surely he must know that Philip was not her type? Although now she came to think of it, what was her type? She had once thought that a kind, patient considerate person like David would be her ideal partner. If so, why had she fallen for someone as arrogant and dictatorial as Brad? She tossed the question back and forth in her mind, unable to find a reasonable explanation, until at last she slept.

CHAPTER SIX

LAURA climbed the steps leading into the clinic, walked along the corridor towards Helen's room, determinedly lifting her chin as she tapped the door and entered. As she had expected, Brad was already there, sitting beside Helen, brother and sister laughing over some shared joke. Immediately he saw Laura standing hesitantly in the doorway his smile faded and a curiously withdrawn look took its place.

Helen, however, called out cheerfully, 'Come in, darling. Isn't it wonderful that Brad's here already? Hang up your coat, and let's have a nice cosy chat.'

She was either unaware of the tension that existed between Laura and Brad or deliberately chose to ignore it, decided Laura, occupying a chair on the other side of the bed. It seemed impossible not to notice Brad's complete change of manner at her appearance.

He gave a curt nod, watching her closely, an unfathomable expression in the depths of his dark eyes.

'Good morning, Mr. Stuart.' Her voice intentionally cool, although her heart raced frantically at the thought that she had only to reach out a hand to touch him. 'Hello, Helen. You look wonderful. No need to ask whether you've recovered.'

'Oh, yes.' Her eyes sparkled. 'I had a good night and now that Brad and I have sorted out our differences the future looks rosy. I start my treatment this afternoon.'

'That's marvellous. I'll keep my fingers crossed for you.'

'You too, Brad.' Helen looked at her brother, appearing to observe for the first time the forbidding lines across his brow. 'Whatever's the matter?' Then looking back to Laura, 'You haven't quarrelled?'

'Quarrelled is hardly the word,' said Brad shortly. 'Let's say we had a difference of opinion.' The eyes that momentarily held Laura's were cold and ruthless, but as he turned to Helen his face changed—almost to tenderness. 'It's nothing to do with you, though, so don't get distressing yourself over our affairs.'

'But it does concern me,' protested Helen, her grey eyes wide and troubled. 'Laura is my friend, I don't like to see her hurt.'

'And I am your brother, so where does that put me?'

'You're an arrogant, conceited pig, if you must know. Why do you have to treat everyone as though they're your inferiors?'

'That's not true.' His smile did not quite reach his eyes. 'If you must know I caught Laura in what I can only term as compromising circumstances.'

'I don't believe you,' exclaimed Helen, as if it was the last thing she would expect of her friend. 'Laura, what's he talking about?'

'Philip,' said Laura grimly. 'He called last night. Brad came in and immediately jumped to the wrong conclusions.'

'Typical,' sniffed Helen. 'He never does stop to weigh up a situation. Believes the worst of everyone. Of course,' her voice heavy with sarcasm, 'he's a paragon of virtue himself.'

Brad snorted. 'There's no need for that, Helen. I know what I saw and Laura didn't deny it. In fact she gave the impression of being more than just friends with— er—Philip. Red roses, my best whisky, the lot.'

'Good for you, Laura,' laughed Helen delightedly. 'I'm looking forward to meeting Philip when I'm better. He sounds quite a guy. Trouble with you, Brad, you're too narrow-minded. You live in a world of your own. I don't suppose you'd ever think of giving a girl flowers —probably a book on the life of the African elephant, or some such rubbish.'

Surprisingly, to Laura at least, Brad looked considerably abashed. 'You make me sound thoroughly disagreeable, Helen. I'm not sure I like it.'

'Well, you are, most of the time. Now, why don't you say you're sorry and offer to take Laura out for lunch? You'll have to be out of here by then, anyway.'

'Oh, no,' interrupted Laura in sudden consternation. In the circumstances the idea of spending an hour or two in Brad's company was more than she could bear. 'I mean, I'm sure Mr. Stuart has other more important things to do.'

Brad raised a cynical eyebrow and for one brief moment Laura thought she saw a flicker of amusement cross his face. 'I quite understand you would prefer Philip's company.' He spoke brusquely. 'But as there are several things I wish to discuss I think it might be a good idea.'

Laura glanced to Helen for support, but the other girl was smiling happily.

'Good. I'm glad that's settled, but promise you won't keep on to Laura, Brad? She's too good a secretary and a friend for you to lose—you said so yourself—and that's what's going to happen if you shout at her all the time.'

'I never shout,' said Brad, his voice rising, then with a wry smile, 'at least not without provocation. But to please you we'll call it a truce, eh, Laura?'

Amazed at his reaction, Laura was taken unawares.

'Y-yes, of course.'

'You don't sound very sure.' This time there was a definite twinkle in his eye. 'Perhaps you'd prefer to go back to the flat?'

'No. Lunch out will be fine.' At least in the impersonal atmosphere of a restaurant she would be less likely to give away her true feelings, which in the close confines of the flat would be virtually impossible. I wish I were an actress like Helen, she thought, then I would be able to hide my feelings more easily. I remember Father saying my face is like an open book.

'In fact,' Brad continued, 'I've changed my mind and brought some work for you to do. You'll never cope if I leave it all until you get home.'

Home! thought Laura. How beautiful it sounded and how wonderful it would be if she could really regard Leastone Hall as her home. She had already fallen in love with the house and the district and to live there permanently would be sheer bliss.

'I've put all my work on tapes. Never liked the gadgets before, but it will save time and trouble—I suppose you have had some experience at audio-typing?' Laura nodded and he carried on sardonically, 'Of course, I should have known that the estimable Miss Templeton is capable of anything.'

'Now, Brad,' Helen cut in, 'don't forget your promise. I *do* wish you and Laura could get on together, but you seem intent on making fun of her. Don't you know she doesn't like it?'

'Helen!' protested Laura.

'I don't care. He treats you abominably.'

'And have you seen the way she treats me?' asked Brad ironically. 'She's not afraid to answer back, if that's what you're thinking. Proper little firecracker she is,

must be something to do with the colour of her hair.'
His eyes rested for a moment on Laura's gleaming head.

'Good for her,' retorted Helen. 'I'm glad you don't get away with everything.'

'Please,' interrupted Laura heatedly. 'Will you please stop discussing me as though I'm not here? As Bad says, I'm quite capable of sticking up for myself. There's no need for you to defend me, Helen.'

Brad threw back his head and laughed. 'See what I mean?'

This only served to incense Laura more, but she bit back a retort and concentrated on picking an imaginary speck of dust from her skirt.

The meal progressed much better than Laura had anticipated. Brad seemed to be taking his sister's words to heart and was pleasantly agreeable, until suddenly Laura heard Philip's voice a few tables away. Afraid to look in case he saw her, Laura questioned Brad about the work he wanted doing. Anything to keep his attention fixed on her, for she knew only too well what his reaction would be if he saw Philip. But he must have realised that there was something wrong, for he frowned slightly.

At the same time Philip saw them. Appearing oblivious to the fact that he might not be welcome, he hailed Laura loudly and sauntered across to their table.

'This is a surprise.' He looked from Laura to Brad and then at their empty cups. 'How about joining me for a drink?'

Laura held her breath as Brad gave him a coldly condescending stare. 'How you have the effrontery to speak to me after last night's little episode I do not know. But as you're here perhaps you'd like to give me your version? I seem to recall you had precious little to say for yourself at the time.'

'Brad!' Laura had expected some reaction, but nothing like this.

He lifted a hand. 'No, Laura, I insist.'

'So you didn't believe me?' Her voice was small, hurt, but so also was her pride, and after glaring defiantly at her employer she turned to Philip, hearing herself say, 'I'd be pleased to accept your invitation.'

What made her speak like this she did not know. She only knew that Brad had hurt her and some inner force compelled her to retaliate. A drink with Philip was the last thing she wanted, but there was no backing out now, whatever Brad might be thinking.

Philip seemed all at once unsure of himself, but after looking hesitantly at Brad he pulled back Laura's chair.

Brad's face was inscrutable, only the tightening of his lips gave away the fact that he was annoyed, and the steely glint in his eyes. 'If that's your decision, Miss Templeton, I'll leave you in the—er—capable,' with a slight lift of his eyebrows, 'hands of your friend. I'm returning home this evening, so I'll put the dictaphone and typewriter in my flat before I go. Please post the work to me as soon as you've finished.'

She was dismissed. Once again her impulsiveness had led her into trouble. As she followed Philip she desperately wanted to find comfort in tears. The last look that Brad had given her was one of utter loathing and she felt as though her heart had broken into a million tiny pieces.

'Come on, snap out of it. It isn't the end of the world.' Philip's voice reached her as if from a distance as she started at the amber liquid in her glass. 'Anyone would think you were in love with the fellow.' Something in her expression must have revealed her feelings, for he continued, 'I say, you're not?' and as she nodded, 'He isn't worth it. He obviously doesn't care two hoots about you.'

Laura smiled, a tiny rueful smile. 'I know, but I can't help it. That's what makes it worse.'

'Now me,' said Philip lightly, 'I'd fall over backwards to have you feeling like that about me. I suppose I'll have to resign myself to being second best—a shoulder to cry on.' Suddenly perceptive to her emotions, he said, 'Would you rather leave? We'll go for a drive, if you like, then you can give way to those tears I know you're holding back.'

Laura nodded again, not trusting herself to speak. This was a side to Philip she did not know. A side she had never suspected existed. In one way she was glad he knew, it would prevent him making any untoward advances, but his sympathy was more than she could stand and before long tears streamed uncontrollably down her cheeks.

He passed her his handkerchief, driving swiftly until they were out of the city, eventually pulling up in a lay-by which ran a little way off the main road.

By this time Laura's sobs had subsided and she managed a watery smile. 'You must think me all kinds of a fool?'

'Don't be silly. All women need a good cry now and then. I have a sister who's for ever coming to me with her problems, so you see I'm used to such scenes.'

He took the handkerchief from her and gently wiped beneath her eyes. 'Your mascara's run. You should use the waterproof kind.'

in an attempt at cheerfulness.

'How do you know about such things?' asked Laura

'My sister again. I can see you don't believe me, but it's true.' He leaned forward and kissed the tip of her nose. 'How about trying to repair the damage? Then we'll drive on for a few miles until you feel ready to return to the flat. We can make a day of it if you like. I've nothing else to do.'

'I think I'd like that,' replied Laura slowly, searching in her handbag for make-up and comb. If she went back to the flat there was the possibility of bumping into Brad, and she wanted to avoid that at all costs. To see again his contempt for her apparently thoughtless behaviour was more than she could take. His aggressiveness, his superiority, she could stand—but to be the subject of his hatred was unthinkable. Her heart was a tight, painful ball. Why, oh, why did she always let Brad assume the worst? If she had allowed him to handle the situation in his own way there was the chance that they might still be friends, whereas now it was impossible to see them ever reaching an amicable relationship.

During the few days Laura resolutely kept herself busy. Her visits to the clinic were confined to mornings only, a period she looked forward to immensely as Helen was so bright and cheerful, so optimistic about being able to walk again. Laura deliberately refrained from telling her about the scene with Brad. It would only mar her present happiness and could do no good. Indeed, knowing Helen as she did, she would probably tackle her brother the next time he telephoned, and that would only make matters worse.

In the afternoons and evenings she concentrated on Brad's typing. At first the sound of his voice as it came over the tape, deep and clear, upset her considerably. It brought back all the emotions she was trying to forget.

But eventually she assumed a professional detachment to his voice and the work became just another job.

The worst times were when she was in bed. Then there was no escaping his presence. How could she forget when she was lying in his bed? When her head lay upon the pillow used so many times by him? These were the times when she gave way to the misery in her heart. Tears flowed unchecked and very often it was the early hours before sleep eventually released her from her wretchedness.

She saw no more of Philip. He telephoned regularly, but Laura refused to see him, using the excuse that she was far too busy. He accused Brad of being all sorts of a slavedriver, but Laura remained adamant. It would be so easy to turn to Philip in this time of despair. Although he was now aware of her feelings for Brad she felt sure he hoped there was still a chance for him. He had turned out so differently from her first impressions, but in all fairness she could not use him as a substitute for Brad, and that was what it would amount to.

One evening a week later Laura was feeling particularly tired and decided to go to bed early. The telephone rang as she was falling asleep, startling her into wakefulness. Annoyed at being disturbed on one of the rare occasions when sleep was coming easily, she padded through to the lounge and snatched up the receiver. There was only one person likely to ring, she decided, and that was Philip with another of his repeated requests.

'What on earth do you mean, ringing at this time of night?' she said crossly. 'Getting me out of bed!'

A slight pause, then a brittle demand: 'Is that how you normally answer the telephone, Miss Templeton?'

Laura's heart skipped a beat, then plummeted to the

depths of her stomach. Why was he phoning at this hour? Perhaps he wanted to apologise? she thought hopefully for one glorious second. But no, he wasn't the type to say he was sorry for something like that. There must be something wrong with the work she had sent.

'Mr. Stuart—I'm sorry. I wasn't expecting you.'

'Obviously,' drily. 'What I have to say won't take long—then you can go back to bed. I didn't realise you were such an early bird.'

His voice mocked her, drew forth a quick retort.

'Surely I'm at liberty to go to bed at any time I like? I don't have to answer to you for that as well?'

'Now you're being childish. That boy-friend of yours has done little to sweeten your temper—in fact I would say that you're more touchy now than before. What's the matter? Isn't your romance running smoothly?'

Furiously Laura gritted her teeth. She would have derived much pleasure at that moment in slapping him across the face. As it was she contented herself with being icily polite. He would probably be more cynical if he knew the effect his words were having.

'My private life is no concern of yours. What was it you wanted me for?'

She heard his swift indrawn breath and waited for the next outburst, but his voice when he spoke was perfectly controlled. Although it was not difficult to imagine the tightening of his jaw, the grim lines round his mouth.

'I'm leaving for Africa in the morning, and I shall probably be away three or four weeks. I tried to ring Helen, but she was asleep, so will you tell her that I'm sorry I couldn't see her again before I left.' His voice softened slightly. 'So that she'll know I've not deserted her—and tell her that I shall expect to see her walking when I return—that should encourage her.'

Laura felt as though a cold hand clutched her heart. With Brad out of the country what chance was there of them resolving their argument? She realised now that she had subconsciously hoped that the next time they met things would be different. To be the object of his derision was more than she could stand.

'Miss Templeton!'

'Yes?' Her voice was small and shaky.

'Did you get my message?'

'Y-yes. I'll tell Helen tomorrow.'

'Are you all right?' A note of concern. 'You sound different.'

'I'm fine, thank you.' in contrast to her previous sentiments she was now glad that he could not see her face, for surely her distress must be apparent?

'Then get back to bed,' he said kindly. 'I hope you haven't been overworking. You're certainly getting through those tapes quicker than I expected. Take a break now. I shan't give you any more work until I return, then I shall begin another book.'

'Yes, Mr. Stuart.' His unexpected kindness made her feel worse than ever and her voice was a mere whisper.

'Good-night then, Laura, and remember this—no man's worth making yourself ill over. No matter how much you love him.'

The line went dead and Laura was left clutching the telephone as though it were a lifeline. A link with the only man she had ever truly loved.

Slowly at first tears rolled down her cheeks, but as she walked back into the bedroom sobs shook her body. He thought she loved Philip! How wrong he was. Her heart and soul belonged to him—would always belong to him even if she were never to see him again.

Once again it was many hours before she slept, and then she was tormented by dreams of Brad. Brad as he had been the day they walked round Shrewsbury. Brad when he kissed her. Brad at his sparkling best.

She awoke the next morning feeling both physically and mentally exhausted. Her reflection in the bathroom mirror revealed heavy shadows beneath her eyes and an unusual pallor to her skin. Aware that Helen would instantly detect any signs of fatigue and undoubtedly comment upon it, Laura skilfully applied extra make-up. The effect was definitely worth while, she decided later, when no comment was made at all on her appearance, unless it was the news that Brad was going to Africa that occupied Helen's attention.

'Not more research!' she groaned. 'How thoughtless at a time like this. He knows I like him to phone me regularly, even if he can't come. It's a good job you're here or I'd go out of my mind.'

'No, you wouldn't. You're doing marvellously. You've managed a few steps now, so it won't be long before you're as good as new.'

'It's so unlike him, though,' she persisted. 'He usually has these things planned for weeks beforehand and tells me over and over again where he's going and how long he'll be away. He must have made up his mind on the spur of the moment.'

She looked so miserable that Laura felt it time to change the subject. 'Tell me about your life in the theatre? I wish I'd known you then—I could have come to see you.'

Once engaged on her favourite subject Helen forgot her earlier disappointment and by lunchtime was flushed and happy, bidding Laura a cheerful good-bye.

Laura walked slowly down the steps of the clinic, head

bent, pondering over Helen's statement that Brad did not usually go haring off at such short notice. He must have had a reason, but exactly what Laura could not imagine. She would have thought, as Helen did, that his sister's health was of prime importance at the moment. Certainly more significant than a trip five or six thousand miles away.

Suddenly she heard a car horn, a voice calling her name. Philip waved from the open window of his Triumph, parked at the kerb. 'Come on, I'll give you a lift.'

Laura hesitated only for a moment, then went towards him. It was time she forgot Brad, she determined. What point was there in hankering after a man who could scarcely be bothered to be civil to her most of the time, when here was another one more than willing to take his place?

As a consequence she put on her brightest smile and when he leaned over to open the door for her the warmth of his welcome was like a tonic. He caught her hands tightly, studying her face. 'You look tired, sweetheart. What have you been doing?'

Laura turned her head away from Philip's perceptive gaze. 'I haven't been sleeping too well.'

'I don't need to ask why,' he said. 'Have you seen him lately?'

She knew it was no use pretending and shook her head. 'He telephoned last night. He's on his way to Africa now.'

'Good,' beamed Philip, and when Laura looked at him reproachfully, 'Perhaps I might see more of you now. He can't give you any work if he's not here—unless that was an excuse not to see me? I'd practically given up hope of you ever agreeing to go out with me again

—that's why I'm here now.'

His smile turned to wretchedness. He looked so sorry for himself that Laura took pity on him and squeezed the hand that still enfolded hers. 'I really was busy, Philip.' That at least was true. He need not know that she had decided that if she could not have Brad's company she did not want to see anyone else. 'But if you like you can take me for a drive—I could do with a change of scenery.'

Her words caused his smile to return and he settled back happily into his seat. 'Let's go,' he said, 'before you change your mind.' He released the handbrake and the car shot forward into the line of traffic.

Laura snuggled down and relaxed. It felt good to be appreciated, even though he could never take Brad's place. Philip was a much nicer person that she had at first imagined and she felt a genuine regret for the way she had treated him. However, he did not seem to hold it against her, keeping the conversation deliberately light in order to make her forget her problems.

The powerful car soon ate up the miles and before long they were in the open country. 'I know a nice little place a few miles further on where they do a superb steak. I don't know about you, but I'm starving!'

'I'm not really hungry,' admitted Laura, 'but—' realising the futility in protesting, 'perhaps something light.'

He grinned. 'We'll see. It's my bet you haven't had a good meal in days. Leave it to Uncle Philip. We'll soon have you restored to good health.'

Unable to resist his infectious humour, Laura smiled back, and it was with a considerably lightened heart that she sat down to her meal a short time later.

After that Philip waited for Laura most days when

she left the clinic, and gradually their friendship deepened. Although she still yearned for Brad—and knew she would do so for the rest of her life—she was able, under Philip's charm and single-mindedness, to push her feelings into the background. Little by little the hurt became less until she could think of Brad without the terrible pain that had at first seared her thoughts. He made no attempt to contact her, or even mention her in the frequent postcards received by Helen. So little did she mean to him, thought Laura, in one of her moments of despair.

Then came the day Philip asked her to marry him.

She had invited him back to the flat for an evening meal—the first time she had dared do so since the day of Brad's untimely intervention. After eating they sat on the settee listening to records. Soothed by the soft music, Laura relaxed at Philip's side, her shoulder touching his, feeling happier than she had for a long time. Before she realised what was happening his arm came round her, the fingers of his other hand tilting her chin gently but firmly towards him.

His kiss was light, experimental, pioneering the way towards a deeper, stronger emotion which Laura sensed was waiting to be unleashed. She alone held the key. The slightest encouragement on her part and the passion throbbing within him would be freed. Appreciating the unfairness of the situation, yet loath to hurt Philip by rejecting his advances, Laura allowed herself to submit to his embrace. Perhaps his kisses would kindle some spark of emotion, arouse a feeling of which she was yet unaware. But no magic existed, no shower of sparks burst overhead as had happened when Brad's lips touched hers. It would not be fair to encourage him further, decided Laura, to raise false hopes. Gently she placed a hand against his chest, feeling as she did so the quickened heart beats, and pushed herself away.

'Philip,' she whispered, 'I . . . you . . .'

'Sweetheart.' He placed a finger against her lips. 'Hear me first. I know you love Brad, but you must also know that I love you. Your kisses now—does it mean you care for me a little?'

'I've grown very fond of you Philip, but—'

'Then marry me, sweetheart,' he cut in earnestly, his face only inches from hers, blue eyes pleading.

'But I don't *love* you. There's a world of difference between liking and loving,' she replied quietly but determinedly, even though deep down she could see this as a way of solving her problem. She didn't doubt for a minute that Philip would make her happy, but to marry without love? It didn't seem right. She loved Brad and if she couldn't marry him was it fair to consider marrying someone else?

'You will—given time,' Philip was assuring her. 'I'll teach you to love me.'

'Philip, I can't. It wouldn't be fair under the circumstances.' Her eyes troubled, Laura clung to Philip's hand.

'At least promise me you'll think about it. I know I've sprung it on you rather suddenly.' One arm still lay across her shoulders and he pulled her to him, kissing her soundly before allowing her to answer. 'Perhaps that will help you make up your mind?'

Laura smiled thinly. Her mind was already made up. But to please him she nodded. 'All right—but don't raise your hopes too much.'

For the rest of the evening and during the days that followed Philip went out of his way to win Laura's love. Flowers and chocolates frequently arrived at the flat. Almost always he appeared outside the clinic to take her home or out for a meal. He made no further reference to his proposal, but Laura knew he was impatient for her decision.

The day of reckoning came when he was waiting outside the flat as she left for the clinic one morning.

'Hop in,' he said, laughing at her astonished face.

'But I'm going to see Helen.'

'I know. I'm coming with you. And afterwards we're going to your favourite restaurant and you're going to give me your answer. I've waited long enough.'

Obediently Laura slid in beside him. 'I don't seem to have any choice. You have it all worked out.'

'True,' he replied. 'If I wait for you I'll get nowhere.'

Laura smiled wryly. 'You've been very patient, Philip.' Indeed he was what had once been her conception of the ideal man—tolerant, kind, thoughtful. She had already decided to tell him that her answer was no, but suddenly she found herself wondering whether to change her mind. After all, if she had never met Brad there would be no hesitation. She sighed deeply, aware that Philip gave her a curious look. It was a difficult decision, one she wished she did not have to make.

And then, five minutes later, as she introduced Helen to Philip, her mind was unexpectedly made up for her. She only had to see the way he looked at Helen—his eyes never leaving her face—and Helen hanging on to his every word, to realise that here was a mutual attraction. They were drawn together as if by a magnet and Laura knew that for most of the morning her presence was forgotten. Occasionally they would remember and bring her into the conversation but they soon became wrapped up in a world of their own again.

Laura felt happy for Philip. He deserved a greater love than she could ever offer and Helen would be so right. It made her wonder why she had never thought of bringing them together before. Philip with his flamboyant personality and Helen with her love for a gay social life. They should go well together.

At one o'clock as they prepared to leave, Helen invited Philip to come again, then turned to Laura, her face glowing. 'He's all you said he was, and more. I wish you'd brought him before.'

'I didn't arrange it today,' smiled Laura. 'He invited himself. But I'm glad he did—for your sake.' She was glad too that she had never told Helen that Philip had asked her to marry him. Now Helen need have no qualms about developing a friendship with Philip.

Outside in the car Philip tried to look as though nothing had happened, starting the engine and heading out towards the suburbs.

'Philip!' said Laura hesitantly, after they had travelled a few miles in silence. 'There's no need to wait. I can give you your answer now and I think you know what it will be.'

'I'm not a mind-reader,' he laughed, but she noticed the way his fingers tightened their grip on the steering wheel as he waited for her to continue.

'Then you should be. I told you once my answer was no, and it's still the same. I haven't changed my mind.'

She heard his breath whistle softly through his teeth, his fingers relaxed their hold. Philip did not realise that she had observed his reaction, but it gave her the proof she needed.

'You're not saying that because of—Helen? I know how it must have seemed to you, but it makes no difference. I've asked you to marry me and—'

'No, Philip, I couldn't marry you. Not loving Brad. It wouldn't be fair.'

'If you're sure that's your only reason? I must admit I find Helen very attractive, but I'm a man of honour. You should know that.'

'I appreciate your kindness, Philip.' Laura laid a hand on his arm. It would never do for him to know how near she had come to saying yes. 'And I hope you'll find true happiness with Helen.'

He gently squeezed her hand. 'Thank you. You're quite a girl. Brad doesn't know what he's missing.'

Over their meal he confided how much this meeting with Helen had affected him. 'I've never felt like this over anyone before,' he admitted. 'I thought I loved you —indeed I still do—but this is different.'

'I know what you mean,' Laura sympathised. 'It's happened to me, don't forget. We don't ask to fall in love. One moment there's nothing and the next, wham, you're in love up to your neck.'

'I only wish you had as much chance with Brad as I appear to have with Helen,' he said ruefully. 'I feel guilty at being so happy.'

'Don't be silly,' said Laura, absently stirring her coffee. 'Snatch your happiness while you can. I'll be all right. I shall probably look for another job when Helen leaves the clinic. If she remains in London I don't fancy being alone with Brad in that great house.' Not if he continues to be unfriendly, she added to herself. A few kind words are all I ask. It would be sufficient to keep me there—fool that I am to even think of it.

After Philip had taken her home Laura found difficulty in settling to any work. Their conversation had crumbled her carefully built defences. For the first time in ten days she was tormented by thoughts of Brad.

Listening to his voice on one of the tapes she burst into uncontrollable tears.

'Why do I have to love you?' she whispered aloud.

Without warning she felt the earphones being lifted from her head and a large soft handkerchief thrust into her hand. A chill ran down her spine. There was only one other person who had a key to the flat. Had he heard her involuntary words?

CHAPTER SEVEN

SLOWLY Laura lifted her head and through her tears saw a misty outline of Brad, tall and forbidding. Her first impulse was to fling herself into his arms, confess that it was he she loved. But then the memory of their last meeting returned. Humiliation that he had caught her in this moment of kindness took its place and in her discomfiture she took refuge in anger.

'How dare you enter without knocking? Surely I'm entitled to a little privacy?' She rose and faced him, dabbing angrily at the tears which still fell.

In the face of this onslaught his thick brows drew together, his jaw tightened. 'I did ring, but as I got no answer I assumed you were out.' He paused, his voice changing subtly. 'I'm sorry if I interrupted something. Would you like a shoulder to cry on? I told you no man's worth breaking your heart over.'

Without stopping to think that he really might be feeling sorry for her, Laura read only derision in his words. Completely oblivious to the fact that he was her employer, or what the consequences of her rash action might be, she lifted her hand towards his face. Instantly her arm was caught in a vice-like grip.

'Let me go.' She tried to twist free but to no avail. The more she pulled the tighter his grip became and now he was actually laughing.

'You're quite a little firecracker, you know that? What's the matter? Don't you like me finding out your secret?' His face loomed ominously close, dark eyes alight with mockery.

Completely incensed, Laura sank her teeth into his hand. 'Why, you little—' he gasped, but she was free and far too indignant to realise what she had done.

'If it will make you feel any happier,' she blazed, 'Philip has asked me to marry him—so please don't waste your sympathy.'

His eyes narrowed. 'You don't exactly give the impression of a happy bride to be.'

'Oh, go to hell and take your damned job with you.' The words were out before she could stop them. He looked at her in stunned silence, then swiftly turned on his heel. The next moment she was alone.

Her legs trembled so violently she could hardly stand. Crossing to the drinks cabinet Laura poured herself a brandy, then limply subsided on to the nearest chair.

Do you know what you've done? she rebuked herself. You've just talked yourself out of a job and a home. The best job you're ever likely to get. Now what are you going to do?

The effects of the brandy steadied her thoughts and the dreadful consequence of her heated action hit Laura with full force. She could apologise, she supposed, beg his forgiveness. But no, her chin came up determinedly, she couldn't ask any favours. She realised that she had been extremely rude, but a stubborn pride held her back. She may as well go now—make a clean break of it. To stay would only end up in more heartache.

Tomorrow she would look for rooms and then ask Mrs. Jennings to send the rest of her clothes on. Fortunately she had not touched last month's pay cheque, so she would have sufficient money to see her through until she found another job.

Unable to face the thought of food Laura retired

early to bed. Staring at the ceiling, her hands folded behind her head, she wondered what had prompted her to tell Brad about Philip's proposal. As before she had deliberately led him to believe that there was something between them. Why, she could not imagine, except for a crazy impulse to hit back when he needled her. He would never know how much she wanted to feel his arms about her, to enjoy the ecstasy of his kisses and hear his whispered words of love. It was a dream that would never come true. She was best away from him.

She had at one time thought it would be sufficient to be near him, content in the knowledge of her love, but now she knew that this could never be so. Her love had made her more vulnerable and his harsh words hurt her deeply. Although Brad was not aware of this fact, her true feelings carefully hidden beneath a façade of indignation, she knew she would be unable to keep up this hostility—sooner or later her true feelings would show through. She shuddered at the thought of his amusement, his patronising manner when he discovered she had followed in the same footsteps as her predecessors. It wouldn't be long after that before he would ask her to leave. She could see it all too clearly. Mrs. Jennings' words, that they either left of their own accord or were sacked, returned vividly to her mind. It was far better that she left now, like this, than have to suffer the ignominy of being fired.

She slept fitfully, waking in the early hours with a throbbing headache. Recalling that she had seen a bottle of aspirin in the bathroom medicine cabinet, Laura padded through and swallowed two tablets down with a glass of water.

The lounge clock said six-thirty. She deliberated whether to go back to bed or take a shower and begin sorting out her things. There was Brad's work also to be put in order, and a half-finished tape to be typed. No matter how she felt, her conscience forbade her to leave without completing the work he had given her.

She had bathed and dressed, eaten a light breakfast of toast and tea and was nearing the end of her typing when the doorbell rang, loud and insistent. Whoever it was he sounded impatient. Probably Philip, she thought, wanting to make sure I'm up. He must be eager to see Helen again.

She withdrew the bolts and opened the door, her mouth falling open and colour staining her cheeks when she saw Brad. Why had he come? To tell her that she was to leave today? What other reason could there be for such an early visit? It was just after eight.

Unsmiling and tight-lipped he faced her.

'C—come in,' she said at last when it became clear that he was waiting for her to speak. 'I—I'm just finishing off your work.'

'I don't think that will be necessary,' he said, following her into the lounge.

She looked round quickly. His eyes were hard like chips of granite. Laura's heart sank. So he wanted her to go immediately. He must hate her very much. Yet his voice had been kind. There was no hint of aggression in the way he spoke.

Their eyes met for a second before she wavered and looked away, but not before his discerning gaze noticed her wan face and shadowed eyes.

'You slept badly.' It was a statement, not a question.

Laura shook her head briefly. 'I have a headache, that's all.'

He looked across at the half-finished page in the typewriter. The completed work neatly piled to one side, then back to Laura who waited, wondering what to expect.

'Sit down,' he said shortly. Laura obeyed automatically, as though she were a puppet and he held the strings.

'I realise that you may have acted hastily last night,' he said, pacing up and down in front of her, his hands clasped behind his back, 'and in a way it was my fault for walking in on you as I did.'

What was he getting at? thought Laura curiously, wishing he would come to the point.

'But you do realise that you're still under contract to me? I'm sure you're not a woman to go back on her word.' He looked at his hand. She could see the marks where her teeth had drawn blood. 'So I'm prepared to forget what happened. You will carry on until the end of your three months. After that you may leave or stay as you wish.

Laura looked at him, amazed. To be honest with herself she hadn't given her contract a second thought, but the condescending way Brad now spoke made her blood boil. If he thought he was doing her a favour by agreeing to forget her behaviour, he could think again. She would stay, of course, until her contract expired, but not a moment longer.

'Very well, Mr. Stuart,' she said woodenly. 'I'll stay until the end of December, but after that you'll have to find yourself another secretary—and—' she twisted her fingers together nervously, 'I'm sorry for being so rude.' She did not feel like apologising after the way he had spoken, but as he himself had attempted to make amends she felt it was the least she could do.

He appeared to be surprisingly pleased by her words, though she was not sure whether it was the fact that she was staying, or leaving at the end of the year, that pleased him.

'Good, that's settled. Now, do you think you could make me a cup of coffee? Then we'll be on our way.'

'I'll make you a drink,' she said, 'but I'm sorry, Philip has arranged to pick me up at nine.' She was glad of the excuse. The close intimacy of a car journey, no matter how short, was one thing she wanted to avoid at this moment. Although he had agreed to forget her rudeness there would inevitably be a strained atmosphere, so the less they were thrown together the better as far as she was concerned.

'Philip!' Brad uttered the word sharply, as if wondering how his name had entered the conversation. 'He's going to the clinic?'

'Y—yes. He came yesterday for the first time—no one objected.' Although she knew from the look on her employer's face that had he been present he would have had plenty to say about it.

'Not even Helen? You know how she feels about anyone seeing her. I should have thought you would have had more sense than to take him.'

'On the contrary,' replied Laura coolly, 'Helen seemed to find Philip very good company. I think she enjoyed his visit. He can be very entertaining.'

'Mmm. We'll see. I'm very pleased with the progress she's making and I don't want anything to upset her at this stage. Hurry up with my coffee and I'll be off. No sense in hanging around.'

He drank the coffee scalding hot and when he left the flat felt empty. Laura wandered aimlessly from room to room waiting for Philip, wondering whether she was destined to find true happiness. The only man she had ever really loved did not seem to even be aware of her as a woman. She was a good worker and he valued her as such, even to the extent of excusing her ill-mannered outburst which no self-respecting secretary would have allowed to happen, but it seemed that anything else was out of the question. She would have to resign herself to this fact whether she liked it or not.

Philip arrived promptly at nine and on the way to the clinic Laura told him that Brad had returned from Africa.

'And how are things between you?' he enquired, slanting her a worried glance.

'We've reached a kind of truce at the moment,' she said, wondering how best to tell him about their quarrel and the fact that he was involved.

'You don't sound very happy about it,' said Philip. 'What's he been saying?'

Laura laughed, but there was no joy in her heart. 'He came in unexpectedly last night. We had a most unholy row and I told him what to do with his job.'

'Good for you,' Philip replied heartily. 'I never could understand why you stuck it. What are you doing now, looking round for somewhere else? My offer still stands if you need it.'

'Thanks, Philip. But you see, he came round this morning and reminded me I'm on contract to him. I'd forgotten all about it.'

'So you're back where you started?'

'More or less,' agreed Laura.

'Oh well,' said Philip philosophically, 'things may turn out better this time. And if you need someone to confide in there's always me.'

'Thanks, you're a darling.' Laura gathered her bag and gloves together as they approached the clinic. 'I don't know where I'd be without you.'

And still she hadn't told him he was supposed to be engaged to her!

Helen's smile widened as they entered, but Brad's face resumed the forbidding lines to which Laura was becoming accustomed. He nodded curtly and Laura heard Philip whisper, 'Chin up, old girl,' before brightly saying, 'Good morning, Helen—Mr. Stuart. Had a good trip?'

'Yes, thank you,' came the brief rejoinder.

In contrast to her brother, Helen appeared to be in the best of spirits. 'Isn't it marvellous, Laura, Brad coming back so soon? Everything's happening at once. I was walking when Brad came. I couldn't believe my eyes —I was expecting you and Philip.' She laughed, the musical sound filling the room. 'Brad thought he was seeing things, too. All of a sudden it feels great to be alive, and I owe my thanks to you two.'

She held out her hands to Laura and Brad.

Laura felt embarrassed at being linked so closely with her employer, but he was smiling fondly at Helen, apparently unaware of his secretary's discomfiture.

'It does us all good to see you like this,' he said. 'It's something I've hoped and prayed for so long that it seems like a miracle.'

Laura, listening to the deep voice which softened affectionately as he spoke to his sister, felt an unreasonable pang of jealousy. She knew how ridiculous it was to resent him speaking to Helen like that, but when her whole body cried out for a gentle glance or a few tenderly spoken words, she no longer cared that it was his sister to whom he spoke. She only knew that she wished with all her heart that the words were directed towards her.

Suddenly aware of Philip's warning glance she pulled

herself together, forcing a smile, and spoke encouragingly to Helen. 'How about letting us all see how well you're progressing? Philip and I are dying to see you on your feet.'

Taking his cue from her Philip said, 'Here, take my arm.'

Helen flashed him one of her lovely smiles. 'Sir Galahad himself, but thank you, I can manage.'

She eased herself to her feet and slowly walked the length of the room and back again. Her face was pale and she appeared to be in considerable pain as she neared her chair, but waving off Philip's ready arm she successfully finished her chosen course.

'Bravo,' cried Philip. 'That was terrific. Sure you haven't overdone it?'

'I'll be all right in a minute.' Helen's breast heaved as she fought for breath. 'That's the furthest I've walked in one go.'

Philip's concern was obvious and Laura noticed Brad slant a puzzled look in his direction. It was easy to guess what he was thinking. In order to distract his attention she caught Philip's arm, saying quietly, 'I'm sure Helen could do with a cup of tea, and I know I'd love one. How about exercising some of your charm on the nurses and seeing what you can do?'

Philip patted her hand affectionately. 'Good idea, sweetheart. Leave it to me.'

When he had gone Helen turned to Brad. 'I can't understand why you don't like Philip. I find him perfectly adorable.'

'It seems most women do,' replied Brad drily, looking at Laura. 'But as I'm not a woman I'm afraid I don't share your enthusiasm. He strikes me as a lazy young scoundrel who doesn't know what it's like to do a hard day's work.'

'Don't be so disparaging,' pouted Helen. 'He must do something, or where would he get all his money? Laura tells me he has his own flat and a flashy car. He wouldn't get those for nothing.'

'Precisely,' said Brad. 'But how and where his money comes from is another story.'

'Surely it's no concern of yours what Philip does with his time,' cut in Laura, unable to reason why Brad should hold a grudge against Philip.

'Of course,' drawled Brad. 'I'd forgotten you're engaged to him.'

For a breathless moment silence filled the room. Laura caught a glimpse of Helen's stricken face before it set into an impassive mask.

'Darling, you didn't tell me,' she purred, looking deliberately at Laura's left hand.

Brad, who had missed his sister's first reaction, echoed her silent question. 'Yes, I wondered where the ring was. Can't he afford to buy you one?'

'It—it happened so suddenly we haven't had time to choose, that's all,' said Laura defensively, careful not to let his taunting words antagonise her.

'Mmm.' Brad stroked his chin. 'I wonder.'

Helen had lapsed into silence, and looking at her Laura knew she was hurt, and blamed herself for not foreseeing that something like this might happen. The trouble was now that if she told Helen the truth she was quite likely to tell Brad that Laura loved him in the hope that it might do her some good. Laura knew from one or two things Helen had said in the past that she cherished the idea that one day Brad might ask Laura to marry him. An idea Laura knew could never materialise.

At that moment Philip returned triumphantly bearing a tray of tea, which he placed on a low table at Laura's side.

'Philip,' Helen spoke loudly, before anyone else could speak. A shade too loudly, thought Laura. 'Why didn't you tell me congratulations were in order?'

Laura's heart lurched uncomfortably as Philip frowned. 'What do you mean? What am I supposed to have done?'

'Hark at the man,' mocked Helen. 'Don't tell us you've forgotten you're engaged to Laura?'

'Of course he hasn't, have you, darling?' Laura flashed him a pleading look as he turned a puzzled face towards her, regretting more than ever the impulsiveness that had led her into this situation. She was aware of Brad eyeing them keenly and breathed a sigh of relief when Philip pulled her arm through his, saying;

'Er, no, but I thought we agreed to keep it a secret, sweetheart.'

She smiled briefly, thankful that Philip had risen to the occasion but realising that he must be wondering what it was all about.

'Then it's my fault,' Brad's dark voice interrupted their conversation. 'Laura told me last night—but she didn't say anything about it being a secret. I do apologise if I've let the cat out of the bag.'

Laura knew he was mocking and it took every ounce of self-control to prevent herself from answering back. She would have given anything to retract the hastily-spoken words of yesterday evening. 'I'll pour the tea,' she said, glad to hide her face. She would have to think up some plausible excuse to tell Helen. Any upset now could impair her chances of complete recovery. According to Doctor Jorgensen the patient's full co-operation was vital in such cases and it was just possible that this unfortunate piece of news could cause a serious setback.

Although Helen's smile was as warm as ever when Laura passed her tea, Laura could sense the other girl's hostility and inwardly quaked. It seemed as though she was fated to be the target of hatred by the Stuart family, and it was not a very pleasant feeling. She was glad when at last it was time to leave.

'I'll take you home,' offered Brad as they emerged on to the street. 'I have some work I wish to discuss— with your permission, of course,' looking directly at Philip.

'Be my guest,' replied the younger man, 'I can't claim her company during working hours. I'll ring you this evening, Laura.'

To Laura's embarrassment he took her face between his hands and kissed her soundly, whispering as he did so, 'Must keep up appearances.'

'If you're sure you can bear to be parted,' broke in Brad bitingly, 'we'd better be on our way. I have other business to attend to.'

A tangible silence filled the car as they made their way through the busy London traffic, but Laura was determined not to speak unless Brad himself opened the conversation. She was annoyed by his attitude towards Philip. There was no call for his sarcasm, and her temper was at such a pitch that the slightest provocation would cause her to say words she would later regret. It was her own fault that Philip had been drawn into this awkward situation and it was now up to her to solve matters the best way she could, and arguing with Brad was not going to help. Consequently the whole of the journey was completed without a word being spoken, and Laura felt distinctly uncomfortable as they entered

Brad's flat.

'Shall I prepare a meal?' she enquired after hanging up her coat. 'You must be hungry after such an early start.' At least he could not accuse her of inhospitality, thought Laura, even though she hoped he would refuse. Brad in this mood was hardly the ideal luncheon companion.

'No, thanks. I already have an appointment, so if you don't mind I'll quickly go over a few details and then leave you in peace.'

He unlocked his briefcase and withdrew a pad of scribbled notes, explaining how he wanted them set out. 'It will be easier for me to work from them if they're typewritten,' he said. 'Don't worry if you can't read every word. I wrote them in a hurry, but I'd like some of them by tomorrow. I'm returning home in the afternoon and I want to start work on my book right away.'

At the door he paused, turning. 'I hope you know what you're doing as far as that young man's concerned,' he said gruffly. 'But I'd like you to know that I've reconsidered the matter, and if you want to get married I'm prepared to release you from your contract.'

'Thank you, but that won't be necessary,' said Laura distantly. 'I wouldn't dream of letting you down.'

He threw her a frigid glance. 'Sarcasm doesn't become you, Miss Templeton. I'd stick to that temper if I were you, anger is far more in keeping with that red hair of yours.'

If there had been a cushion handy Laura would have thrown it, but as it was she contented herself with turning her back and walking steadily into the kitchen. She heard the door slam and the roar of his engine as he drove away.

What an infuriating man he was, she thought, vigorously whipping an egg. He certainly knew how to bring out the worst in her, and what was more seemed to enjoy it, otherwise why would he deliberately taunt her? She found herself wondering what it would be like to spend a few hours in his company without quarrelling. She had done, in what seemed now the far distant past. Was it really only two months ago? It was incredible to think they had spent an whole afternoon together without a cross word. In those days, although Brad had still been arrogant and masterful, he had seemed to enjoy her company. He had never deliberately attempted to embarrass her as he did now. In fact it was only since Philip appeared on the scene that he had altered. Could—could he possibly be jealous? Laura dismissed the idea immediately it was born. It was ridiculous. He could hardly be jealous of Philip if Laura herself meant nothing to him, unless he were envious of the other man's easy charm and natural friendliness towards women in general. Yes, she decided, that must be the reason for his increased moodiness. He's realised he isn't the charmer he once thought he was.

She spent the afternoon trying to decipher the hieroglyphics which represented Brad's notes, and by the time Philip telephoned at seven she was glad of the respite. Her head ached through prolonged concentration, and when Philip suggested eating out she willingly agreed, although she realised that his sole reason was probably to find out how he had become 'engaged' to her.

'I don't fancy bearding the lion in his den,' laughed Philip. 'Or shouldn't I say that?'

'You can say what you like about him at the moment,' returned Laura, 'I've had enough of Brad Stuart for one day.' It was a blessing Philip didn't sound angry, she thought. It was lucky he had played along so well this morning, but he must be full of curiosity.

They went again to the Golden Crest and in the convivial atmosphere of her surroundings Laura slowly relaxed, feeling the tension of the last twenty-four hours gradually leaving her body.

'That's better,' smiled Philip, as she laughed at a joke told by the comedian. 'It's the first time you've laughed today. Perhaps you can now tell me how it is I've assumed the role of your fiancé without even knowing it—you've not changed your mind?'

Laura had been waiting for the question all evening, trying to think how best to tell him, but now that the moment had arrived her heart hammered painfully. All her carefully rehearsed speeches fled and she blurted out, 'No—no, it's not that. But—I'm sorry—but in a fit of temper last night I told Brad that you had asked me to marry you—what I didn't tell him was that I'd refused.'

While explaining Laura had concentrated on stirring her coffee, but as Philip did not reply she looked up, surprised to see his body shaking with quiet mirth.

'You're not annoyed?'

'On the contrary, I think it's hilarious. I wish you'd told me sooner, though. I nearly failed you this morning.'

'You did admirably,' said Laura. 'But what are we going to do now?'

'Whatever you want, my sweet. I'm game to carry it through for a while i fit suits your purpose, though what you hope to gain by it I can't imagine.'

'But what about Helen?' Laura was still deeply concerned for her friend. 'I know there's a mutual attraction between you, and it must have been an awful shock when Brad said we were engaged, even though she managed to hide her feelings very well. If we tell her the truth I'm afraid she will blurt it out to Brad—with the best possible intentions of course—but I'd rather he didn't know just yet,' bitterly, 'it will only give him something else to add to my list of failings.'

'Mmm,' frowned Philip. 'It's quite a problem. Leave it to me. I'll think of something. How much longer is Brad likely to remain in London?'

'Until tomorrow afternoon.'

'I see. It will mean Helen suffering another day thinking you're my fiancée, but then I can put her out of her misery, poor girl.'

Relieved that the matter had been taken out of her hands Laura flashed Philip a grateful smile, unaware of how beautiful she looked and the fact that Philip was thinking what a fool Brad was not to see that Laura was eating her heart out for him.

The opportunity to tell Helen came earlier than expected. Philip picked Laura up as usual at nine the next morning and when they reached the clinic Brad had not yet arrived. Helen was still in bed, looking pale and tired, and Laura knew that her fears of yesterday were not unfounded.

'Darling,' said Philip in concern, crossing immediately to her side. 'What's the matter? Aren't you well?'

'You should know.' Her voice was bitter, sulky, not unlike the one Laura had heard her use to Brad the day she overheard them quarrelling.

'There now, my dearest. I know what you're thinking, but it's not true, so you can stop feeling sorry for yourself.'

For an instant a ray of hope shone in her eyes as she looked from Philip to Laura. But it immediately disappeared and Laura was shocked at the despair which took its place. 'It must be true,' Helen asserted. 'Brad wouldn't lie, and anyway *she* told him.'

Laura cringed at the venom in Helen's voice, but Philip took her hand and whispered soothingly, 'Listen, Helen. It was all a story made up for Brad's benefit. Laura's trying to make him jealous, don't you see? But you mustn't tell.'

Laura opened her mouth to protest, but Philip, anticipating her action, held up a warning hand. Biting her lip anxiously she watched Helen, who now seemed more cheerful but still eyed Laura warily. 'Why should Laura want to make Brad jealous?'

'Because she loves him, silly.'

'Philip!' protested Laura hotly, unable to control her tongue any longer. What on earth did he think he was playing at? He was telling Helen the very facts that Laura wished to keep quiet.

Ignoring her interruption Philip said, 'So you see, Helen, it's a little secret between us.'

Helen's face relaxed into a smile, then she laughed and nodded. 'Laura—you're a dark horse, why didn't you tell me?'

'Because I was scared you'd say something to Brad and he must never know I love him—not unless he—he —but no, that's out of the question. Promise you won't say anything, Helen?'

'Of course I won't. Cross my heart. I know he thinks a lot of you, so if this doesn't make him realise what an opportunity he's missing I don't know what will.'

Inwardly Laura fumed at the embarrassing situation in which Philip had placed her, but as Brad arrived at that moment all talk centring round her engagement was curtailed.

Brad was in a surprisingly good mood, and even when Laura told him that there were several sentences in his notes that she had been unable to read he remained unperturbed, declaring he would probably be able to remember them anyway.

He remained for little longer than an hour, during which time Laura noticed him constantly watching her, an unreadable expression in his dark eyes. She found his attention disconcerting, convinced that he had guessed there was some mystery surrounding her engagement and that he was trying to find out what it was.

When he departed Laura relaxed a little, but as soon as she and Philip were alone she wasted no time in tackling him with the question that had worried her all morning. 'Philip, what on earth made you tell Helen how I feel about Brad? I trusted you.'

'I couldn't think of any other reasonable explanation,' replied Philip in concern. 'I decided that to take her into our confidence and pretend it was all a big secret was the only way to get out of it.' He grinned encouragingly. 'You do love him, anyway.'

'Yes,' flashed Laura, 'but that wasn't the reason I told Brad you'd asked me to marry you, and well you know it. If I could take back the words I would—look at the mess I'm in now.'

'He won't find out, unless you tell him,' smiled Philip, apparently unmoved by her anger.

'It's Helen I'm bothered about. If she decides she can help by telling him, then she will. I know she promised, but—'

'You're wrong, Laura,' broke in Philip. 'I know I've only just met Helen, but I've got her weighed up pretty soundly. She'll enjoy sharing this secret.' He took a hand from the steering wheel and squeezed Laura's arm affectionately. 'Forget it now. I wish I could take you out to lunch, but today I have a business appointment—

don't look so amazed—I do work sometimes.'

He drew up outside the flat. 'See you in the morning. You'll be all right?'

Laura nodded, trying her best to smile. She didn't share Philip's optimism regarding Helen. It would be dreadful if Brad ever found out her true feelings when he himself had little or no regard for her. She waved good-bye and reached for her keys.

It was difficult to believe that Helen had really fallen for their story. It seemed to her that if Brad believed she was engaged to someone else he would be even less likely to take any interest. In fact, now she came to think of it, her position was worse than before. There was not the slightest chance of their friendship developing. Brad would never get himself involved with someone else's girl—that much she knew. It was a matter of completing her contract and looking for another job. Hard though the break would be, she knew it was the only way.

CHAPTER EIGHT

AS Laura and Philip entered the clinic the next morning, they met Helen walking along the corridor towards them.

'Darlings,' she said, 'guess what? I can go home tomorrow. Isn't it wonderful?'

'The best news in the world,' said Philip, enfolding her in his arms and whirling her round. 'Except for one thing.'

'And what's that?' demanded Helen, as if wondering what could possibly mar this happy moment.

'I shan't see so much of you. My work keeps me here.' He tucked her arm in his and led the way back to her room, Laura following.

Helen's news had caused her heartbeats to quicken. Tomorrow they were going home! To the house she had grown to love. If only she could look forward to a welcome from the master of the house she would be as excited as Helen. But that was more than she dared hope.

Aware that the other girl was speaking, Laura dragged herself back to the present.

'How about you, Laura? You haven't said much. Aren't you glad to be going back?'

'Of course I am! And I'm awfully pleased for you, Helen. Does Brad know yet?'

'No. I wondered whether you'd drive us home, Philip, then we can surprise him?' She clapped her hands excitedly. 'I can just imagine his face when he sees me walk into the house. Please say you can.'

Philip smiled fondly. 'I've no doubt it can be arranged. Fortunately I've a very capable manager.'

'Manager?' queried Helen. 'What sort of work do you do?'

'I own a nightclub,' and as the girls expressed surprise, 'I inherited it from an uncle who's let it run down, but after a lot of hard work I'm glad to say it's raking in the profits. I can afford to relax a little now.'

'The Golden Crest?' Laura recalled the way his appearance had demanded attention—and her assumption that it was because he was a regular customer. And then she remembered something else. His reason for negotiating with David Greg. He had wanted a huge publicity campaign for the re-opening of the Golden Crest. She recalled it clearly now. It was funny she hadn't recollected it when he took her there, but somehow she had never associated him with being the owner of the place. When he placed the order with David, it must have been three or four years ago, she had assumed he was merely an employee carrying out instructions.

'The very same,' smiled Philip.

Helen's face glowed with excitement. 'How marvellous. I can see now why you're free most days. This is one in the eye for Brad—he thought you were one of the idle rich. I'm glad he's wrong.'

'I may be rich,' he said, 'but I'm far from idle, although I suppose it could appear that way to someone who doesn't know.'

'Why haven't you mentioned it before?' asked Laura. 'Fancy taking me there and not even admitting that you own the place.'

'You never asked what I did,' laughed Philip. 'But

135

seriously, some people get the wrong impression. They seem to think the worst of you for some obscure reason —ignorance, I guess—so unless I'm asked I rarely mention my work. Now, Helen, what time do you want me to pick you up tomorrow?'

'Any time,' she replied with a shrug. 'Eric's very sweet. He wanted to let Brad know, but I soon persuaded him otherwise.'

'Eric?' frowned Philip.

Helen laughed. 'I do believe you're jealous. Eric's my doctor. I've known him for a long time.'

'I see. I think I'll go and have a word with him,' adding in reply to Helen's startled gaze, 'in case he has a message for your brother.'

As the door closed Helen turned to Laura. 'I expect you're nearly as pleased as I am to be going home? I knew you'd fallen for Brad, even though you wouldn't admit it, not even to yourself.'

'Was it so obvious?' Laura asked wryly.

'Only to me, I've seen the signs before. I don't know what it is about Brad that appeals to women, but I suppose that's because he's my brother. Now Philip, he'd never treat his women the way Brad does.'

Laura smiled. 'He is rather sweet, I agree.'

'I was horrified when I thought you were engaged to him,' said Helen, examining her nails. 'I wanted to scratch your eyes out.'

'I'm sorry. I didn't think Brad would tell you.'

The other girl looked at Laura intently. 'Somehow I can't see you doing a thing like this. Are you sure it wasn't Philip's idea? It sounds much more like him.'

'In a way it was,' said Laura, adding quickly before Helen had time to probe any further, 'Would you like me to pack your case?'

'You can help, if you like, but I'm looking forward to doing things for myself again. Eric says the more exercise I get the quicker I'll be back to normal—and the sooner I'll be back in London,' she finished quietly.

Laura looked at Helen anxiously. 'You're not staying with Brad?'

'Not on your life. Once I've been given a clean bill of health I'll be away. I'm bored to tears in the country. Lift my case down, please, and we'll sort out my clothes.'

When Philip returned the two girls were in the middle of packing, clothes strewn over the bed and chairs, looking as though they would never all fit into her one suitcase.

'I must go now, Helen,' he said. 'There are one or two things to sort out before I leave. I'll pick up Laura in the morning and we'll be here about nine. Will that suit you?'

He kissed her cheek as she nodded and clung to him for a second, and Laura swiftly turned her attention back to the suitcase. Seeing Helen and Philip together emphasised the loneliness in her own heart. If only Brad would look at her like that, instead of with the cold contempt he usually handed out. But the fault was her own; she had spoilt any chance of friendship in that direction, and must remain content with whatever happiness she could find.

The journey back to Leastone Hall was accomplished in high spirits. Helen sat in front with Philip while Laura occupied the back seat, sometimes listening to their light-hearted chatter, at other times wondering what the future held in store. It wouldn't be too bad while Helen was there, she decided, but later the outlook was definitely bleak.

They halted for lunch towards the end of the journey,

and afterwards Helen suggested Laura sat in front. 'If Brad sees us arrive he'll wonder what *I'm* doing there,' she smiled. 'Mustn't spoil your little game.'

As it was they were out of the car and approaching the heavy door before it was flung open and Brad, followed by Mrs. Jennings, came rushing down the steps.

'Helen! Why didn't you let me know? This is better than I expected. I wish you'd telephoned, though, I'd have fetched you myself.'

'Surprise, surprise, Brad darling,' she laughed, 'and Mrs. Jennings, what do you think of me now?'

'It's a miracle, Miss Helen.' Tears streamed unashamedly down the housekeeper's cheeks. 'I never thought I'd see you walk again.' She put her arms round the younger girl and hugged her soundly. 'Now let's get you inside out of the cold.'

Brad smiled indulgently at her proprietorial attitude and stepped back for Laura to precede him into the house, giving her a cool smile as he did so. She heard him thank Philip for his trouble, adding that it hadn't really been necessary, and Philip's flippant reply that he'd thoroughly enjoyed escorting two pretty girls a hundred or so miles.

They gathered in a little group in the hall. 'Oh, Jenny,' began Brad, as if suddenly remembering there was a stranger in their midst, 'this is Philip. Philip—er?'

'Harvey,' supplied Philip, throwing the housekeeper one of his winning smiles.

'Laura's fiancé,' finished Brad abruptly.

'You never said you had a young man in London,' reproached Mrs. Jarvis, looking at Laura. 'Will he be staying the night?'

'Of course he will,' interrupted Helen. 'He can't drive all that way back today. You don't mind, do you, Brad?'

'How can I refuse my dear sister when she smiles at me like that?' said Brad lightly. 'You're welcome to stay, Philip. Mrs. Jennings will put you right.' His smile did not quite reach his eyes.

'Very kind of you.' Philip caught Laura's hand and drew her towards him. 'I'm glad we can have a few more hours together. I couldn't bear the thought of being parted so soon.'

Laura smiled through gritted teeth. Surely it wasn't necessary for him to carry their engagement fiasco to such lengths? She could feel Brad's disapproval as he turned away towards his study.

'If you'll excuse me, I have work to do. I'll see you all at dinner.'

Helen grimaced at his retreating form, waiting until his door was properly closed. 'Big brother disapproves,' she said irreverently. 'Come on, let's get washed and changed, then we can show Philip round the house.'

About an hour before dinner Helen announced that she was going to lie down, and for the first time since their arrival Laura was alone with Philip.

They sat before a blazing log fire in the drawing-room, the green velvet curtains drawn against the cold evening air.

'Did you have to behave like that in front of Brad?' she accused.

'Must keep up impressions,' Philip replied lightly, 'or what's the point in going on with this lark?'

'I still think it was unnecessary.'

'You really are upset,' he said in concern. 'I can't understand Brad, he must go round with his eyes shut. Do you want to call the whole thing off? He may look at you in a different light if you're free.'

'I doubt it. We didn't get on before. Besides, I couldn't

lie to him, and if I told him the truth he would probably tell Helen that you really did propose to me. She wouldn't like that. Let's leave things as they are for the moment.'

He looked at her doubtfully. 'As you wish, but don't go and spoil the evening by resenting my attentions. Brad will think there's something strange if I don't make a fuss of you.'

'I'll try,' said Laura sadly. 'Now we'd better go and change.'

They stood up and Philip placed his hands lightly on her shoulders. 'Keep your chin up. There's plenty of other fellows if he's not interested.' He kissed her lips softly and for a second Laura clung to him, aware of her need for sympathy. She never heard the door open, she heard nothing until Brad's smooth voice startled her.

'I'm sorry to interrupt such a charming little scene. I thought Helen might be here.'

Laura pushed Philip away hotly, feeling unreasonably guilty at being caught in his arms.

'She's resting. She felt tired after her long day, but she said she'll be down to dinner.'

'I see.' He glanced at his watch. 'I hadn't realised it was so late. Shouldn't you be getting ready? Jenny hates unpunctuality.'

'We were just going,' put in Philip laconically, 'but I couldn't resist giving Laura a kiss. She's so beautiful, don't you agree?'

A muscle tightened in Brad's jaw as he gave Laura a searching look. 'Indeed she is. You're a lucky man. I'll see you later.' His face inscrutable, he turned and walked out, closing the door quietly after him.

Laura threw Philip an angry glance and made to follow, but he caught her arm, turning her round to face him. 'Now don't get on your high horse. You dragged me into this game, and to tell you the truth I'm enjoying it. Before I leave Brad's going to realise just what a wonderful person you are.'

'Philip! Don't you dare. I thought you were my friend.' Green eyes flashed indignantly.

'So I am. All I shall do is give a little push now and then in the right direction. The way Brad just looked at you, it was as though he was seeing you for the first time. With a little help he'll soon realise what he's missing. Leave it to Uncle Philip.'

Laura smiled. 'I can't be mad with you for long, but I'm warning you, if you show me up—I'll—'

'You'll what?' he laughed into her eyes. 'You won't do anything. You'll be too scared.'

'Don't be so sure,' retorted Laura, twisting free and opening the door. 'I'll see you later.'

She changed into a long blue dress that clung warmly to her slender figure. If Philip really intended to show her off she would need that extra bit of confidence. Carefully she smoothed in pearl eyeshadow and mascaraed her lashes. For once she would wear her hair loose, she decided, and brushed it vigorously until it shone like pure copper.

With one final satisfied look at herself in the mirror she snapped off the light and went quietly downstairs.

Brad and Philip were already in the dining-room, talking softly together by the fire. Her footsteps were cushioned by the deep carpet and she was able to observe the two men before they became aware of her presence.

Brad, tall and dark and incredibly handsome in a grey suit and white shirt accentuating his tan, which had deepened noticeably during his visit to South Africa. He was relaxed and confident, very much the master of the house, and Laura's heart somersaulted wildly as she allowed herself to study him. He boasted not an ounce of superfluous flesh. His shoulders were broad, his waist narrow and he carried himself proudly. He was smiling now at something Philip had said, his eyes crinkling at the corners, his mouth softening.

Swallowing a sudden constricting lump in her throat, Laura turned her attention to Philip, blond and much shorter, wearing a check suit; equally as confident as Brad but with the ease and familiarity of a younger generation. Looking at him now, Laura could see why Brad's first impression had been unfavourable. Indeed, she herself had once thought him a smooth talker, out for what he could get. It was only as she got to know him better that she realised how wrong she had been.

As of one accord they turned and looked at Laura as she stood silhouetted in the doorway, young and graceful and lovely.

Brad's eyes darkened perceptibly and he took a step forward, but it was Philip who spoke. 'Here you are,' he said, 'looking more beautiful than ever, if that's possible.' He kissed her warmly, then held her at arm's length. 'You should let your hair down more often, it suits you. What do you think, Brad?'

Laura's eyes flashed warningly, but Philip appeared not to notice.

Slowly, almost insolently, Brad looked her up and down, lingering on the rich auburn hair which fell provocatively across her face and shoulders, finally looking deep into her eyes. Laura felt uncomfortable under his gaze but, determined not to let him have the satisfaction of finding out just what effect he had on her, she assumed what she hoped was a casual air.

'Philip, darling, I'm sure Brad's not interested how I

wear my hair.'

'On the contrary,' cut in Brad blandly, 'I find it very appealing. Now, would you like a sherry?'

He turned away as if bored by the whole affair and Laura found difficulty in swallowing back the tears that threatened. He didn't have to make it so apparent that he had little time for her. Was it such an effort to be polite? If so why hadn't he let her go when she wanted to, instead of reminding her of her contract? Admittedly he had said he would release her if she wanted to get married, but she had the feeling that he'd done that purely as a matter of form, not prompted by any personal feeling of guilt that he might have.

Philip, sensing her emotion, squeezed her hand encouragingly. She smiled weakly, realising that she would be letting him down if she spoilt the evening by allowing her own sentiments to show.

'Just a small one, please,' she said brightly.

'I'm not too late, am I?' Helen's cheerful voice relieved the tension and Laura turned gratefully.

'No, I've only just come down myself. How are you feeling?'

'Wonderful. I'm a completely new person, thanks to my darling brother.'

Brad glanced at her fondly. 'You didn't think that at the time.'

Helen looked at him innocently. 'I didn't? How very naughty of me.'

He laughed as he handed her and Laura their drinks. 'We'd better sit down. I can hear Jenny.'

Once again Laura felt an irrational spurt of jealousy at the carefree relationship that existed between brother and sister. It was stupid, she knew, but it was a feeling over which she had no control. She wanted him to speak to her with the same effortless repartee, to laugh over shared jokes, not to be the object of his derision and contempt.

Despite Laura's apprehension, the evening was a success. Whether it was Jenny's excellent cooking or the mellowing effect of the sherry Laura did not know, but Brad was certainly more agreeable than she had known him for some time.

Helen, too, radiated a deeper happiness which Laura knew was because of her love for Philip, but which Brad assumed was due to her almost complete recovery. Once or twice Laura caught a lingering look passing between her two friends and each time her heart skipped a beat, for fear Brad saw and wondered.

Philip seemed to have forgotten his desire to impress Brad with her qualities, for which Laura was thankful, and when Helen said she was tired and intended retiring early, he surprised them all by saying :

'Me, too. If I've to drive back to London tomorrow I must get a good night's sleep.'

Laura panicked inwardly, suspecting an ulterior motive behind this decision. He had previously told her that he needed little sleep, so his excuse was feeble to say the least. If he thought any good would come of leaving her behind with Brad he was mistaken. She would follow their lead and go to bed herself.

'I'll come with you,' she said, 'I feel rather tired myself. It must be the travelling. Good-night, Brad.' She turned to follow the others.

'Laura!' Brad called her back. 'I'd like a word with you before you go, if it's all right with Philip?'

'Of course,' said Philip jovially. Too jovially, thought Laura. It sounded almost as though he was pleased to leave her there. She threw him an imploring glance but he continued, 'I'll just kiss her good-night—then she's yours.'

He took Laura into his arms and kissed her soundly. She felt her colour rise and would have liked nothing better than to slap him hard across the face, but such an action would reveal the fact that she did not really love him. She was forced to pretend to enjoy his kisses, muttering between clenched teeth as he released her, 'You wait!'

He smiled broadly, immune to her wrath. 'Good-night, sweetheart. See you in the morning. Come on, Helen, I'll help you upstairs.'

He closed the door gently behind him and Laura turned to find Brad watching her, amused. His unexpected attitude caused her to divert her anger from Philip to him and she spoke without thinking:

'I really don't know what you find so funny in my fiancé kissing me good-night. Perhaps he should have asked your permission?'

'Or yours?' countered Brad softly, quizzically.

'W-what do you mean? Of course he doesn't have to ask.' His question had caught her off guard and she felt confused. What was he getting at?

'I may be wrong, but I distinctly gained the impression that you didn't welcome his embrace.' He watched her closely, waiting for her reply.

'How would you feel?' she demanded hotly. 'I prefer my kisses in private, not in front of—of strangers.'

He frowned. 'I hardly think you can class Helen and me as strangers. If you really loved the fellow you'd kiss him no matter who was present.'

'Don't be ridiculous,' blazed Laura. 'That may be your opinion, but it's definitely not mine. Love is something personal, to be shared when you're alone.' She was scared that he had noticed things were not quite as they should be between her and Philip, and his next words confirmed her suspicions.

'So you don't care that he finds my sister attractive—so long as he doesn't fuss you in public?' He stood with his back to the fireplace, regarding her gravely.

'Naturally he finds Helen charming,' she said defensively. 'What man wouldn't? She's a very beautiful girl.'

'Agreed, but that hardly gives him the right to openly admire her when he's engaged to you.'

'It's no business of yours,' Laura retorted. 'If I don't mind surely that's all there is to it?'

'You're wrong there. Helen is obviously impressed by Philip—don't think I haven't noticed the way she looks at him—and I don't want him playing about with her emotions when nothing can come of it.'

'Surely Helen's old enough to realise when someone's serious or not? She knows we're engaged.' The conversation was becoming difficult and Laura clasped her fingers tightly behind her back, willing him to change the subject.

'Old enough, yes, but wise enough, I don't know. All I know is that I don't want her getting hurt. She's gone through enough recently.'

'And just what do you propose I do?' Laura lifted her head proudly. 'Tell him I don't want him to speak to Helen again? What would he think then? That I'm jealous? I may have green eyes, but jealousy is not one of my traits.' At least not as far as Philip's concerned, she added to herself. With Brad it was a different matter.

'Now who's being ridiculous? You know quite well what I mean.' His eyes darkened and he took a step forward.

Laura drew back involuntarily, not noticing the table

behind her. Brad came forward another step and placed his hands on the table one each side of her, effectively blocking her retreat, his face within inches of her own. Cold grey eyes looked into frightened green ones.

'Let me go,' she demanded. 'Just what do you think you're doing?'

'Trying to prove something,' he answered calmly, as with deliberate slowness his lips came nearer to her own.

Laura's heart hammered painfully when she realised his intentions, but what reason lay behind his actions she could not imagine. She only knew that it was important not to let him find out the true state of her feelings.

She felt the warmth of his breath against her cheeks and suddenly, breathlessly, twisted her head to one side, pushing her hands hard against his chest. He remained solid, immovable, and she heard a light mocking laugh.

One hand came up behind her back, tangling itself in her hair and pulling her head back sharply. 'Yes, your hair's definitely better this way,' he whispered, then his lips were on hers, crushing, bruising, demanding. It took every ounce of self-control to keep herself from responding, from allowing her heart to rule her emotions. But she succeeded—perhaps too well. For he flung her from him without a sound, returning to lean his head against his arm on the mantelpiece.

The desire to admit her love for him, to wipe away his defeated attitude, which puzzled her greatly, became stronger. With a smothered cry she ran from the room and did not stop until she reached the privacy of her own quarters.

There she lay on the bed and sobbed, allowing her tears to fall freely until at last she felt calmer. Quietly opening the door she looked along the corridor, ensuring no one was about before slipping into the bathroom. She showered and splashed her face with cold water until the redness round her eyes disappeared, but she could still feel the warmth of his kisses and a painful tightening round her heart as she recalled the unleashed passion behind his embrace.

What animal instinct urged him to act as he had? What was he trying to prove? That he could draw more response from her than Philip had? Was that it? If so he had failed and judging by his reaction he had not liked to admit defeat. His pride was probably badly hurt, thought Laura, used as he was to women falling at his feet. Perhaps now he would realise that not all women were the same. This last thought was not strictly true, for hadn't she turned out to be little better than all the other girls before her? Except that she had successfully kept her feelings hidden. She supposed he was piqued because she hadn't conformed to the pattern of the rest of her sex, but at what cost to herself had she resisted his advances? More than she cared to admit, but she didn't intend letting him think that she too had fallen prey to his undoubted good looks and charming manner when he chose to exert it, which wasn't often as far as she was concerned.

Back in her bedroom she lay awake, listening to the sounds of the old house as it too settled down for the night. Outside a strong wind pulled at the branches of the trees, whistling through the tall pines. Suddenly she heard the soft but unmistakable sound of the front door opening and closing. Wondering who could be going out at this late hour, Laura jumped out of bed and pulled back a corner of the long, heavy curtains. At first she saw no one, but as the moon appeared from behind the racing clouds she saw Brad illumined in its ghostly light.

He was standing quite still, apparently intent on something in the distance.

As she watched he turned and looked up, just for a second, and then he walked away into the shadows. Hotly she let the velvet fall. Had he seen her? If so, what would he think? That she too could not sleep? That his kisses had disturbed her? But he couldn't possibly realise how she felt. She was letting her imagination run away with her. Even so, sleep still refused to come. Her mind was with the man out there in the cold, wondering what he was doing, what impulse had caused him to take a midnight walk.

It was a full hour before she heard Brad return and his careful footsteps pass her room. His door clicked gently to and at last, content with the knowledge that Brad was safe, she slept.

Laura woke the next morning with a raging headache. She drew back the curtains and sunlight flooded into the room causing her to gasp and hold a hand to her head as its brilliance hurt her eyes. Stumbling to the bathroom she swallowed down a couple of pills before washing and dressing and making her way downstairs.

In the dining-room Philip sat near the window reading the morning paper. He rose as she entered, his ready smile fading when he saw her white, drawn face.

'Sweetheart, what's the matter? Are you ill?'

'I have a headache,' Laura smiled wanly. 'It will pass.'

Philip held out her chair. 'You look as though you ought to be in bed. Does Brad know you're not well?'

'I've seen no one.' She then noticed that the table was set for two only. 'Isn't he joining us?'

'He's already eaten, according to Mrs. Jennings, and is hard at work. Helen's staying in bed for a while, so we're on our own, sweetheart.'

So Brad had reverted to eating alone, thought Laura. He could at least have waited until Philip had left. After all, he was the host, even though Philip was an uninvited guest. Unless he was being tactful in leaving her and Philip together? She smiled at this thought. Tact as far as Philip was concerned was one of Brad's failings. He made no secret of the fact that he didn't like her friend, and was more likely to intrude on their privacy than arrange it for them. No, he was probably still annoyed with her over last night, she decided. And there was nothing she could do about it.

'What time are you going?' she asked, buttering a slice of toast.

'Straight after breakfast, I'm afraid. I must get back today. Helen's invited me up for the weekend, but I'm tied up; Saturday and Sunday are our busy times. Anyway, I'll try and come soon or Brad will think there's something wrong. I take it you still want to carry on with this charade?'

'Oh, yes!'

Laura's reply was so emphatic that Philip raised an enquiring eyebrow. 'What's he been saying? I thought it strange when he asked to speak to you alone last night.'

'Er—nothing,' said Laura. She had no intention of telling Philip what had happened. It was just possible that he might decide to tax Brad about it and ask him what right he had to interfere in their affairs. 'He wanted to discuss some work,' she said finally, it being the only other excuse she could think of.

She could see Philip did not believe her, but all he said was, 'A funny time of day to talk work. Couldn't it have waited?'

Laura shrugged. 'It's not up to me to question him. He *is* my employer.'

'I keep forgetting that. Sorry. Ah, here's Mrs. Jennings. I'm starving.'

'None for me, Jenny,' said Laura, smiling up at the housekeeper. 'Toast and tea is all I want.'

'You certainly don't look well,' said Mrs. Jennings in concern. 'Why don't you go back to bed?'

And let Brad think I'm scared to see him? thought Laura. 'No, thanks. I'll feel better when the tablets work. It's only a headache.'

'Well, I think you ought to tell Mr. Stuart. You can't work feeling like that,' said the older woman emphatically.

She left the room and Philip looked at Laura. 'She's right. Would you like me to have a word with him?'

'Oh, do stop fussing,' said Laura, beginning to feel annoyed. 'Anyone would think I was really ill instead of a silly headache.'

'Well, you look ill,' insisted Philip. 'But you know best, so I'll shut up.' He attacked his bacon with relish. 'I'll say one thing for Brad—he's got a jolly good cook in Mrs. Jennings. I wouldn't mind a few more of her meals.'

By the time Philip left, Laura's head was not quite so bad. As Brad had not put in an appearance she decided to go and face him. It was already half-past nine.

She tapped on his door and entered. He looked up from his desk—his face stern, eyes cold and expressionless. For a second he studied her, but if she thought he was going to comment on her paleness she was wrong.

He deliberately looked at his watch. 'I was beginning to wonder whether you intended doing any work today?' His voice was low, scornful.

Laura bit back a hasty retort. 'I'm sorry, I was seeing Philip off,' and she could not resist adding, 'He wondered why you weren't there.'

'Some of us have work to do,' came the terse reply. 'We can't all spend our time gadding about the countryside.'

'You seem to forget that he saved you a journey yesterday,' retorted Laura, again stung into retaliation. 'The least you could do was say good-bye.' Immediately the words were out she regretted them.

'Perhaps I thought you'd like to be alone?'

Like hell you did, she thought, more confident than ever that he was put out by her behaviour of the previous evening.

'How very kind of you.' She injected just the right amount of sarcasm into her voice to make him wonder whether she was serious or not. 'If you'll tell me what you want doing I'll start.'

'The work's already on your desk,' he said coolly. She was halfway through the dividing door when he spoke again. 'And Miss Templeton—I'd like it all finished today'.

'Very well,' she said, closing the door. But when she looked at the pile of papers and tapes her lips compressed.

If Jenny and Philip could tell she was not well, surely Brad must also have noticed? She glanced resentfully at the door, tempted for a moment to march in and tell him she was taking the day off. But pride held her back. She would finish no matter what. She had no desire to give him the satisfaction of reprimanding her for falling down on her work.

CHAPTER NINE

DURING the days that followed Brad appeared to delight in finding fault with Laura's work. It seemed as though her engagement had served only to increase his antipathy. But instead of her own love dying by his constant harsh words it deepened, and as the week passed Laura found it more and more difficult to hide her feelings. As a result she became increasingly subdued. She no longer enjoyed their verbal sparring matches and meekly accepted his recriminations. Even Mrs. Jennings commented on her wan appearance and lack of appetite.

The nights were the worst. Lying in bed, Laura's misery engulfed her completely. She slept fitfully, tormented by dreams of Brad. Brad chasing her through the grounds of the house with a handful of letters. Brad kissing her wickedly and then thrusting her away in disgust. And worst of all, a tender loving Brad asking her to marry him.

The morning after this particular dream Laura felt more despondent than ever. There was still another three weeks of her contract left and she wondered how she would manage to get through it. She sat at her typewriter, staring at the distant hills, their summits disappearing into the low-lying clouds, wishing for the hundredth time that she had never taken the job.

How long Brad had been watching she did not know, but a slight movement caused her to look swiftly round, her eyes widening as she saw him standing in the doorway.

For one unguarded moment she thought she saw concern in his dark eyes, but the next instant they were blank—as cold and impersonal as ever.

He walked towards her, studying her face as he did so. Laura felt uneasy under his disconcerting gaze, but lifted her chin determinedly, waiting for the inevitable tirade. What was wrong now? she thought tiredly. No matter how hard she tried she could not please him these days.

'Is something bothering you, Laura?'

His voice was unexpectedly gentle, and Laura wondered at this sudden change. But what could she tell him? How could she say, I love you, Brad. I want you to love me? She bit her lip anxiously as he silently waited.

'N-no,' she lied. 'There's nothing.'

He frowned. 'Don't hedge, girl. I can see for myself the change in you. You're not ill?'

'No. I tell you I'm all right.'

He stood before her desk, his hands planted firmly on the smooth, dark wood. Reluctantly her eyes were drawn to his; she saw that he too looked tired and drawn. It was funny she hadn't noticed before.

'It must be Philip,' he was saying. 'I knew he was a cad right from the start. Gains your affection and then ignores you. Have you heard from him since Monday?'

Laura shook her head, wondering whether it was time to end this nonsense about her being engaged. Then, realising that at least it was a means of escape as far as Brad's enquiring mind was concerned, she decided against it. 'No, but I expect he's busy in the evenings. He owns a nightclub, you know.' If she expected her words to startle him she was disappointed, for he merely raised an enquiring eyebrow. 'And he wouldn't disturb me in the daytime because he knows I'm working.'

'Hmph,' snorted Brad. 'Some excuse, that! If he loves you as much as he makes out he'd ring every day.'

'I really don't see what concern it is of yours how I conduct my private life,' said Laura coolly.

'It is when your work suffers. Don't forget I pay you to do my typing and I expect a reasonably accurate job.'

'I'm sorry,' retorted Laura primly. 'I'll try and see that I make no mistakes in future.'

He gave her one last penetrating look before disappearing into his study, and Laura tried to settle down to work. But Brad's conversation played on her mind and she found it impossible to concentrate. She wished she had not seen that look of concern. It was easier to bear his intolerant manner if she knew he did not care. Why, oh, why had she got herself into such a situation?

Suddenly, desperately, she decided to tell Helen everything. She needed to relieve her bottled up emotions and Brad's sister was the only person. Perhaps after all Helen would not be too upset over Philip's proposal to Laura. It might be that she herself attached too much importance to it owing to her own unsettled state.

Her mind made up, she watched the time anxiously and as soon as it was one o'clock she left her office in search of Helen. She found her in her bedroom sorting through her wardrobe. An open case lay on her bed.

'You're not going?' Disappointment sharpened her words. If Helen left it would be more than she could bear.

'Only for the weekend,' laughed Helen. 'Don't look so worried. What are you doing here anyway? Isn't it time for lunch?'

'There's something I must tell you—in private.'

Helen immediately stopped folding a dress and pointed to two chairs near the window.

'Let's sit down then you can fire away. I knew there was something wrong, the way you've been behaving these last few days. Is it Brad? He hasn't reacted as you thought he would?'

'Partly,' said Laura, taking a deep breath. 'But the truth is when I told Brad that Philip had asked me to marry him, I wasn't lying.'

Helen's face paled. 'What do you mean? What are trying to tell me? That you're really going to marry Philip?' Her voice rose shrilly on these last words and Laura hastened to reassure her.

'No, no. It never came to that. You see I refused him. How could I say yes, knowing I loved Brad? But he asked me to think it over and I was on the verge of agreeing when he met you. I saw straight away how things were between you, and told him then that my answer was still no. I realise now that he never really loved me, Helen. We're very good friends, but that's all, and I hope you won't hold it against him?' she finally pleaded.

The colour returned to Helen's face and she laughed. 'Is that what's worrying you? I love Philip so much that I don't think I care what's happened in the past—but thanks for telling me—you didn't have to.'

'I did,' said Laura, 'for my own peace of mind, but that's not all that's bothering me. I—I don't think I can go on loving Brad and being the victim of his moods at the same time. It's more than I can stand.'

'Poor Laura!' Helen laid an affectionate hand on her arm. 'I wish there was something I could do. Have you told him you're not really engaged?'

'No. I wouldn't gain anything by it, and it's an excuse

for my low spirits. He asked me earlier what was the matter.'

'That's wonderful! It means he must care about you a little,' Helen smiled jubilantly.

'About his work, you mean,' said Laura sadly. 'That's all he's bothered about. No, I don't think I'll tell him yet, unless you and Philip want to get married, and then I'll have to admit to deceiving him. If only I hadn't signed that wretched contract I'd be away now.'

At that moment Jenny popped her head round the door. 'There you are,' she said crossly. 'Don't either of you want any lunch?'

'Sorry, Jenny,' said Helen brightly. 'We're just coming.'

Now that Laura had shared her problems she somehow felt easier, even though she was no nearer a solution. You couldn't make a person love you, no matter how hard you tried. It was a matter of sticking it out to the end, and with Helen to talk to it would make things much easier.

Surprisingly, she ate all her lunch and managed to finish her work that afternoon without making a single mistake.

Saturday dawned and Brad joined the two girls for breakfast.

'I'm glad you're here, Brad,' said Helen. 'I've decided to spend the weekend in London with—with a friend, and I wondered if you'd run me into Shrewsbury? There's a train at eleven.'

Brad frowned. 'Are you sure you're well enough to go gallivanting off? Shouldn't you give it another week or two?'

'Of course I'm all right,' said Helen airily. 'The doctor told me not to sit around all day—which is virtually what I'm doing here.'

'We-ell,' Brad was still unsure. 'There's not much I can say if you insist, but unfortunately it's Jarvis's day off and I'm too busy to take you myself. You'd better ring for a taxi.'

'I'll take you,' interposed Laura hastily. 'I've nothing planned for today.'

'The Mini's in for repairs,' said Brad. 'Unless—do you think you could manage the Jag?'

Laura had never driven such a powerful car and was about to admit her doubts when Helen cut in:

'Of course she can. It's simple to handle. I can put her right if she's in any difficulty and by the time we reach Shrewsbury she'll be used to it—unless,' she looked at her brother archly, 'you'll lend *me* the car and I'll drive to London myself.'

Helen knew what she was doing, for Brad immediately said, 'Oh no, you don't—you're not up to driving yet. Laura can take you.'

Winking slyly at Laura, Helen got up and kissed his cheek. 'Thank you, darling. Come on, Laura, let's get going. I don't want to miss that train.'

They collected their coats and Helen's suitcase and were half way towards the garage at the side of the house when Brad called them. He held a bunch of keys in his hand. 'You won't get far without these,' he drawled sarcastically. Laura felt her colour rise, expecting another caustic comment as she took them from him. She had been used to finding the keys left in the Mini and had automatically assumed the same as far as the Jaguar was concerned.

'Drive carefully,' he said quietly, to her complete amazement, but she doubted whether his concern was for herself. Naturally he was worried about Helen, but he was probably thinking more of his car than anything else, she decided unreasonably.

'I will. I may do some shopping and perhaps go to the cinema this afternoon, if you don't need the car?'

'Of course.' He was surprisingly agreeable. 'Stay out as long as you like.'

She found the Jaguar easy to handle and after the first mile or two felt as though she had been driving it all her life. Helen was excited at the prospect of seeing Philip again, admitting to Laura that she was staying at his flat, and hardly stopped talking about him during the journey.

Laura waited until her train departed, then strolled leisurely round the shops. Christmas was only two weeks away and they were filled with colourful displays designed to tempt the most cautious shopper. Laura wondered idly how Christmas would be spent at Leastone Hall. She couldn't imagine Brad dressing up the old house, or placing a tree in the great hall. He would probably work as usual, she supposed. Her mind slipped back to how it must have been years and years ago, with the house full of children. Presents piled beneath a huge tree, masses of holly everywhere, log fires crackling, laughing voices filling every corner.

Saddened by the changes the old house must have seen Laura felt tempted to buy some of the sparkling garlands and decorations, but remembering that she was only an employee and that Brad more than likely had very fixed ideas on how Christmas should be spent, she contented herself with purchasing one or two presents. A warm woollen scarf and gloves for Jenny, a leather handbag for Helen, a soft mohair sweater for herself. She bought Philip some cuff-links and debated whether to get Brad a present, deciding against it in the end. He was hardly likely to buy her one, and she did not want to cause embarrassment.

She had lunch and then went to see a James Bond film which, despite the fact that she had seen it before, she thoroughly enjoyed. It was dark when she came out, and trying to rain.

As she pulled out of the car park and headed back home Laura wondered how Helen and Philip were getting on. It really wasn't fair to keep up the story of her engagement. She would choose her time and tell Brad the truth; he could say what he liked. After all, it wouldn't be long before she was gone.

Suddenly the car spluttered and coughed and came to a shuddering halt. Laura sat for a moment not fully comprehending what had happened. Then she unsuccessfully tried to start it again. Petrol, she thought, looking at the gauge, but it read half-full, so what then was the matter? The workings of an engine were a mystery to her, but nevertheless she found a torch in the glove compartment and after struggling to lift the bonnet carefully checked to make sure no leads had worked loose. So far as she could tell everything was in order, but the car still refused to start.

With a sinking feeling she weighed up the situation. There were no garages at all on this stretch of road and she could not recall seeing a telephone box. She was isolated, miles from anywhere.

She waited for a while ready to signal a passing motorist, but the road was deserted. Not many people came this way, it seemed, probably using the main road a few miles across country. It was unfortunate for her that Brad had chosen such a secluded place to live and she decided there was nothing for it but to start walking.

It was now raining heavily, and she pulled the collar

of her coat tightly round her neck. Soon her hair was plastered to her head and the stinging rain ran in rivulets down her face. She was cold and uncomfortable and very annoyed. This would have to happen when she used the car, she grumbled, trudging along head bent. Brad would undoubtedly blame her. This was something else he could add to her ill-starred reputation.

Across the fields she suddenly saw a light twinkling. A farmhouse, she thought, or at least some sort of dwelling where she could get help.

Pushing open a heavy gate Laura stumbled through a muddy field in the direction of the light. As she neared she could see that her first guess had been right. A dog barked loudly as she crossed the yard, causing her to look round, startled. In the gloom she did not see the animal beneath her feet; she cried out sharply, feeling a searing pain in her arm as she fell.

'Don't try to move. The doctor will be here shortly.'

The friendly voice reached Laura from a distance as she struggled to rise. Obediently she lay still. A blurred figure gradually came into focus. A plump, homely woman, smothered in a huge flowered pinafore. Laura frowned and looked round. She was on a chintz-covered settee in a comfortable living-room. A fire blazed cheerfully and a dog lay sleeping on the hearth. As she looked he opened one eye, regarding her lazily. Remembrance came flooding back and she returned her gaze to the woman at her side.

'Th-the car,' she said. 'It's broken down.'

'Never mind that now. George will see to it later.'

'But I must let Brad know.' Laura winced at the pain in her arm, feeling a wave of nausea pass over her.

'Later,' soothed the voice, which seemed to get further

and further away, and Laura felt too weak to argue.

It was an age before the doctor finally arrived, a short, stocky man with a tight-lipped smile. He carefully examined her arm, pronouncing to Laura's relief that there were no bones broken. Severe bruising, he said, which would be painful for the next few days, but otherwise she was okay. He gave her some tablets to ease the pain, took her name and address, and then was gone.

Laura sat up as the door closed, feeling stronger now and extremely worried about Brad's car. She looked at the clock ticking loudly on the shelf above the fire. Nearly nine o'clock. He must be wondering what had happened to her.

The plump woman returned carrying a cup of tea. 'Drink this, love, and take two of those tablets.'

'I'm being an awful nuisance,' said Laura. 'I do apologise. I wanted to use your phone. The c-car's down the road. I don't know what's the matter with it.'

'You couldn't drive anyway, with that arm. I'll ask George to run you home in a minute—Leastone Hall, is it?'

'That's right. I work for Brad Stuart.'

The farmer's wife smiled broadly. 'Ah, yes. A nice man. Would you like me to phone him and tell him you're here?'

'Please,' said Laura, pondering over the fact that this woman knew Brad and found him likeable. He must save the aggressive side of his nature for me alone, she thought bitterly, finishing the tea and setting her cup and saucer down on the table.

She was standing by the fire when the older woman returned, staring bleakly at the flames.

'There, I knew he'd be concerned. He's asked George to fetch him—says he thinks he knows what's wrong with the car.'

'Oh dear,' said Laura. 'Was he very cross?'

'Not at all, love. More worried about you than anything else. Don't you think you ought to be sitting down? You look very pale.'

'I suppose so.' Laura sank on to an armchair, aware that her legs were shaking and her heart had quickened its beats at the thought that Brad was coming to fetch her.

And he was concerned about her!

This thought caused her to flush warmly, then the feeling receded, leaving a cold chill round her heart. He couldn't possibly be concerned. Hadn't he shown only too clearly how much he despised her, choosing every available opportunity to let her know this fact?

George's wife kept up a constant stream of chatter and Laura answered at appropriate intervals, but her thoughts were constantly with Brad, her ears alerted for the first sounds of his arrival.

At last she heard the murmur of the Jaguar's engine and its tyres swishing to a halt outside. 'Here they are,' said the other woman, jumping up and hurrying to open the door.

Brad and a tall, ruddy-faced man entered. Laura looked up nervously, wondering what sort of reception she would get. After one quick glance in her direction he turned to the farmer's wife. 'Thank you, Mrs. Richardson, for looking after my secretary, and you, George, for fetching me. This would have to happen when my other car's being repaired.'

'Think nothing of it, Mr. Stuart. Glad to help a pretty lady.' George looked admiringly at Laura.

'If you're ready, we'll go,' said Brad shortly.

It was doubtful whether the Richardsons noticed any

difference in his voice, thought Laura, but she herself had. An ever so slight trace of his former hardness was there and his eyes were coldly impersonal as he watched her rise.

She thanked the farmer and his wife for their help and followed Brad outside to where the Jaguar waited. The car jolted over the cobbles and with each lurch her arm throbbed painfully, but Laura was determined not to let him see her discomfort and shrank back into her corner of the seat, biting her lip to prevent herself from crying out.

Back on the road Brad's voice broke into the silence. 'I'm afraid I owe you an apology.'

Laura looked at him wide-eyed. Brad apologising! What had he to be sorry about? It was she who should express regret for bringing him out on such a nasty night.

'I thought Jarvis had had the petrol gauge mended, or I'd have told you to check. As soon as I heard you'd broken down I knew what was the matter. There was a can of petrol in the boot for such an emergency—although I doubt if you thought of that?'

Laura, who had been considerably moved by Brad's apology, felt a spurt of anger at this last unreasonable supposition.

'Of course I didn't look for petrol when the gauge showed half-full—I did check that—and I also checked the leads and plugs.' Let him think she knew a little about mechanics, thought Laura defiantly. It was just like him to accuse her of ignorance without ascertaining the true facts.

'I see,' he muttered. 'Is your arm very painful?'

A change of tactics, thought Laura. If he hoped this would make her forget her annoyance he was mistaken. 'You're not really concerned,' she grated icily, 'but if it makes you feel any better, yes, it does hurt.'

She felt him look at her. 'I'm sorry,' he said, his voice oddly gentle.

'I'll bet you are,' retorted Laura, determinedly keeping her voice cold, although she could feel herself weakening at the softer tones. 'I can't imagine you feeling sorry for anyone.'

He drew in his breath sharply, and Laura immediately regretted her impulsive words.

'Is that what you think? I know I don't compare very favourably with Philip, but I didn't realise I rated so low in your opinion.'

Laura winced at his biting retort, but knew that if she spoke now she would only make matters worse. She took refuge in silence.

'Frightened to admit it?' he jeered. 'Miss Templeton at a loss for words! I never thought it would happen.'

Fortunately he could not see the hurt on her face, or the tears glistening on her lashes, and the next few miles were travelled in silence. Stealing a glance at Brad, his face faintly visible in the light from the dashboard, Laura noted his compressed lips and tightened jawline, and wished achingly that he would be nice to her—just once. She was tired, oh, so tired, of his cold-hearted manner and harsh words.

Brad pulled up as they reached Leastone Hall, jumped out and opened Laura's door before she had time to touch it herself. Puzzled by his thoughtfulness and wondering what was coming next, Laura slid from her seat and walked beside him into the house.

A worried Jenny waited in the hall. 'Laura, are you all right? I've been worried sick since George Richardson rang.'

'Of course, Jenny. I've hurt my arm, that's all, so silly

165

of me.'

Laura winced as she eased off her coat, not noticing that Brad watched her. The next moment he was at her side helping with deft, gentle fingers. The touch of his hand on her arm felt like fire and she pulled sharply away, certain he would notice her quickened pulse and heightened colour.

He frowned as she withdrew, muttering under his breath, 'You needn't make it so obvious that you dislike me,' and turned away towards his study.

Jenny glanced from one to the other as if aware of the undercurrent lying between them and wondering what it was all about, but Brad closed his door without a backward glance and Laura headed towards the stairs. The housekeeper hastened after her. 'Would you like me to help you undress?' she asked kindly.

'I'll manage, thank you,' said Laura, pausing to smile at Jenny.

'Then I'll bring you up a hot drink. I shan't be long,' and she bustled away towards the region of the kitchen.

In her room, as Laura somewhat painfully undressed, she could still feel Brad's touch on her arm and was oddly puzzled by his attitude. It was almost as though he was hurt by her reaction, but that was ridiculous. She sometimes wished she *had* the power to hurt him, as he so often hurt her. She was still puzzling over this when Jenny came in with hot milk and biscuits.

The housekeeper hovered by Laura's bed, seeming reluctant to leave, straightening sheets and covers which did not need straightening and finally asking the question which had evidently been troubling her.

'I couldn't help but notice that there's something wrong between you and the master. He doesn't blame you for what happened?'

'No,' smiled Laura, 'of course not. It's just—that we don't always see eye to eye.'

'Who does?' said Jenny. 'But it looked more than that to me.' She looked keenly at Laura. 'You wouldn't be falling in love with him by any chance?—Oh, I know you're engaged to your fancy London friend, but I can't see that working out.'

Was her love for Brad so apparent? thought Laura in dismay. If Jenny had noticed, how about Brad? The answer did not bear thinking about; she would have to be more careful in future.

'Me—in love with Brad?' she echoed. 'Why, he makes no bones about the fact that he doesn't like me—I'm only waiting to finish my contract, then I'm leaving.'

'Oh no, miss,' Jenny looked horrified, 'you can't do a thing like that. Whatever would the master do without you? Why, when George Richardson telephoned to say you were hurt, he looked very upset. He had his coat on and was waiting long before George arrived.'

Laura thought about this, and the look on his face a few minutes earlier—then dismissed the idea as preposterous. 'You're wrong, Jenny, I'm sure. It was his car he was concerned about, not me.'

The housekeeper shook her head. 'I only know what my eyes tell me, but then perhaps I imagine things. Is there anything more you'll be wanting tonight?'

'No, thanks, Jenny. I'm all right now,' smiled Laura.

Once the housekeeper had left Laura sipped her milk, her mind dwelling on Jenny's words. Suppose it was true that Brad had been worried about her? The idea was tantalising, yet she could not accept it. Apart from the usual polite enquiry that anyone would make, he had shown little interest in her well-being.

Feeling warmed and comforted by the hot drink and a

little easier now that the tablets were beginning to take effect, Laura slid between the sheets, falling almost immediately into a deep, dreamless sleep.

The weak rays of a wintry sun filled her room when Laura awoke the next morning. She looked at her watch, disturbed to find that it was nearly ten. Why had she slept so late? Why had no one called her? As she tried to sit the pain in her arm told her. It felt so stiff she could hardly move, and she was wondering how she was going to manage to wash and dress when Mrs. Jennings entered, carrying Laura's breakfast on a tray.

'Jenny, you shouldn't! Why didn't you wake me?'

The housekeeper smiled—a smile which seemed to say 'I was right'.

'Mr. Stuart said you're to stay in bed this morning. It's Sunday anyway, so there's nothing for you to do.'

Laura looked warily at Jenny. 'What's made him so thoughtful all of a sudden?'

'I'm not as hard as you might think.' Brad appeared in the doorway and Laura flushed hotly, immediately aware of the flimsiness of her nightdress, trying unsuccessfully to pull the sheets up to her chin.

Amusement flickered across his face, his eyes deliberately lingering on her body. 'I won't stay long,' he said. 'There's nothing worse than cold bacon and egg. I merely wanted to make sure that you obey my instructions.'

Obey his instructions! Laura felt like jumping out of bed. Who was he to say what she should do? He might be her boss five days a week, but today was her own and she resented being ordered about. She looked at Jenny's inscrutable face, back to Brad's half-smiling one, and realised suddenly that she hadn't the strength to get up. His look had turned her legs to jelly, and what was more aggravating, she knew that he was aware of it. She only hoped that he'd put it down to the fact that he'd seen her so immodestly dressed and not guess at the true cause of her feelings.

He spoke again. 'How's your arm this morning?'

'It's very stiff, but I expect it will wear off as I use it.' She looked down, noticing for the first time the purple bruise covering almost the whole of her forearm.

'I think you'd better have a few days' holiday,' he said gently. 'There's nothing that won't wait,' and with that he was gone, leaving Laura extremely surprised by his consideration.

'What did I tell you?' smiled Mrs. Jennings. 'You can't say now that he's not concerned.'

'Probably for your benefit,' said Laura, her mind refusing to accept the fact that Brad could spare a thought for her health.

'Hmph,' snorted the housekeeper as she placed the tray on the bed, 'some people don't know when they're well off,' and she departed, her stiff back displaying her disgust.

After Laura had finished her breakfast she spent the rest of the morning reading, enjoying the unaccustomed luxury of lying in bed. At mid-day she decided to wash and dress ready for lunch. It would take her considerably longer, hampered as she was by her arm.

She was in the hall when the telephone rang. It was Helen. An excited, breathless Helen. 'Guess what? Philip's asked me to marry him. Oh, Laura, I'm so happy.'

'I'm happy for you, too,' said Laura. 'I expect now you want me to tell Brad that—'

'Well, yes,' cut in Helen. 'I was going to ask. You said that if—'

'I know. Of course I'll tell him, I've been meaning to for days. Do you want a word with him?'

'Please. I intend staying here for the rest of the week —I hope he won't put his foot down.'

'I shouldn't think so,' said Laura, and then as Brad came into the hall, 'here he is now.'

As she entered the dining-room she heard his voice raised in anger. Apparently he did object, confirming her decision that he was a most unreasonable man. A thunderous expression on his face, he followed her into the dining-room. The meal was eaten in silence; now was not the time to tell him about her and Philip, she decided. It would only give him another opportunity to vent his anger and irony on her.

After lunch he disappeared and Laura did not see him again that day. The next morning Mrs. Jennings told her that he had gone away for a few days.

Laura's immediate impression was that he had gone to fetch Helen back—until she realised he could not do that. Helen was over the age when he could dictate to her—this was probably what rankled, she thought drily. But it was strange he should leave without saying where he was going. Most unlike him.

Laura spent the week exploring the grounds—weather permitting. When it rained she curled up by the fire with a book, and as soon as her arm felt easier she finished knitting the jumper she had started.

It was Saturday before Brad returned. He seemed in no better a mood and shut himself away in his study. The same happened on Sunday. It was not until after tea, when the front door opened and Helen and Philip burst in, that he emerged to see what the noise was about.

As soon as Helen saw her brother she darted towards

him, waving, her hand in the air.

'Look, darling! We're engaged.'

Brad's eyes glittered like the diamond she held beneath his nose as he looked from her to Philip and finally to Laura.

'I don't think I understand,' he said coldly.

CHAPTER TEN

HELEN clapped a hand to her mouth, looking at Laura in alarm. Barely perceptibly Laura shook her head before saying lightly to Brad, 'Oh, didn't I tell you? Philip and I decided not to get married after all.'

Brad's eyes narrowed. 'I see,' he said slowly. 'At least, I think I do.' He looked across to where Helen now stood holding Philip's hand. 'Congratulations—I think this calls for a drink.' He eyed the younger man guardedly. 'I hope you're sure this time?'

'Oh yes,' said Philip, pulling Helen's hand through his arm and looking at her affectionately. 'I'm perfectly sure.'

They moved into the drawing-room, and after Brad had poured drinks Helen suggested he fetch Mrs. Jennings so that she too could join in their toast.

'I'm frightfully sorry,' she said to Laura as soon as the door had closed. 'I thought you'd told him.'

'I didn't have a chance. But don't worry, it doesn't matter. It was probably easier this way.'

'I expect he thinks me all kinds of a rotter,' said Philip, but Laura could tell by his smile that he didn't really care. He was too much in love to let other people worry him.

Laura kissed him quickly on the cheek. 'I hope you'll both be very happy.'

The evening passed pleasantly, if with a certain amount of restraint on Brad's part, but it was a relief to them all when he excused himself early on the grounds of work.

A little while later Laura herself said good-night, guessing that Helen and Philip would like to be alone for a while. She was surprised to see Brad's study door open and as she passed he came out. 'I'd like a word with you,' he said softly, standing back for her to precede him into the room.

Laura wondered what he wanted that could not wait until morning. She was soon to find out. He indicated one of the armchairs near to the fire, sitting on the other one himself. 'I'm sorry,' he began gently.

Frowning, Laura waited, wondering what he had to be sorry about. He had done nothing to upset her.

'I rather suspected that something like this might happen,' he continued, 'but—you—did you know that Helen and Philip were—?'

'Yes,' nodded Laura. 'And there's no need to feel sorry for me. It's just one of those things.'

'You poor girl,' he leaned forward, taking her hands in his, 'I can see now why you've been so upset recently. You knew all along what was happening, yet you put Helen's happiness before your own. If it weren't for the fact that it's my sister who's involved I'd tell him exactly what I think of him. As it is I want to spare her any more misery, and it's you I'm worried about at the moment.'

He stood up and pulled her to him, his arms sliding round her back and holding her gently but firmly. Laura lifted her head. She must explain. But his lips were on hers, softly, tenderly stemming her words. For one heavenly moment Laura responded, allowing herself to enjoy the exquisite pleasure of his kiss before fully realising what she was doing. Then she pushed him from her with the strength born of desperation, and with cheeks flaming she rushed from the room.

'He can't do this to me,' she whispered achingly as she closed the bedroom door. 'I don't need his sympathy. It's his love I want.' She sank miserably on to the bed. Tears of despair ran down her cheeks, and in her agony she decided she must leave. She could not face the thought of even another day seeing and loving Brad, knowing he would never be hers. Her mind made up, she felt easier, and in the refuge of sleep was able to forget her misery.

When she woke the next morning memory of last night's scene came flooding back, and with it a renewed determination to make today her last one at Leastone Hall. She looked sadly round the room, at the elegant splendour of her surroundings. She was a fool to throw away such luxury; any other girl would jump at the opportunity of a job like this. But her decision was made. There was nothing for it but to leave. She simply could not go on living in the same house as Brad, knowing as she did that the chances of his returning her love were non-existent.

After a solitary breakfast Laura marched determinedly into his study. He looked up, smiling; a smile which set Laura's pulse racing. He looked so handsome and so infinitely desirable. Although he was clean-shaven, a blue shadow persisted on his chin. She wanted to run her fingers lightly down his face, to feel the smooth freshness and inhale his after-shave and the faint lingering odour of Havana.

'Do you feel better this morning?' His deep voice was soft with concern, and Laura felt her resolution wavering.

Please don't be nice to me now, she begged silently, it's more than I can stand. She spoke with more conviction than she felt. 'I'm all right. But—Mr. Stuart—Brad, I want to ask you to release me from my contract. I know there's another two weeks, but I'd like to leave today.' She linked her fingers tightly together, waiting nervously for his reaction.

Gone was his smile. He frowned, yet his eyes remained friendly and his voice still held an element of concern. 'Running away won't do you any good, Laura. Sit down. Let's talk this over.'

Laura obeyed, hoping he wasn't going to make things difficult. Now that her mind was made up she wanted matters finalised as quickly as possible.

'Now,' he said, elbows on desk, fingertips pressed lightly together. 'What plans have you made?—None, if my suspicions are correct.'

'Well—not yet, but—'

'And do you think that you can find suitable accommodation just like that? Especially so near Christmas.'

'I thought perhaps my old landlady would find me a room.'

'You thought! And if she couldn't, what then?'

'I—I don't know. I hadn't got that far.'

Brad rose and walked round his desk, his tall figure looming above her. 'Good gracious, girl,' he thundered, his face now frightening angry, 'have you no sense? Don't you know what could happen to you?' He paced across to the window, staring out for a few seconds; seconds which seemed like minutes to Laura as she sat waiting, hating the thought that he was right and yet equally determined to have her own way.

He turned and Laura checked a cry of surprise at his expression. He looked—almost upset, she thought. His lips were tightly compressed and a pulse jerked spasmodically in his jaw. The shadow on his chin was even more prominent against the paleness of his face.

'No!' His voice was carefully controlled. 'I won't let you go. You signed a contract and I wish you to honour it.'

'Brad, please. What difference will two weeks make?' Laura quailed beneath his penetrating gaze, but faced him bravely. He couldn't, shouldn't dictate to her.

'Enough to make you realise how foolish you are. It was quite obvious to me that you and Philip were never suited, yet here you are willing to ruin your life simply because you've found out he doesn't love you.'

'That was nothing to do with it,' retorted Laura hotly, rising from her chair. 'And anyway, my personal life is no concern of yours. I'm here as your secretary —nothing more.'

He smiled grimly. 'Precisely, and as such I feel morally responsible while you're under my employment —which is for another two weeks—understand? If by the end of that time you still want to leave I'll help you find somewhere to live.'

Laura realised she was defeated; that short of walking out on him there was nothing more she could do. She would have to stick out the next fourteen days as best she could.

He placed his hands on her shoulders, regarding her gravely for a moment or two. 'Be strong, my little autumn treasure. Time is a great healer.'

Laura blinked back the tears that threatened, and smiling weakly slipped from his grasp. 'Perhaps I'd better start work.' If she wasn't careful she would find herself in his arms again, perhaps even admitting her love for him. And what humiliation that would cause! It would put them both in an embarrassing situation.

In the sanctuary of her office she sank her head into

her hands and wept. She wasn't aware that Brad quietly opened the door and watched, did not see the tenderness on his face as he silently withdrew. She allowed her sadness to engulf her until at last she felt better. Two weeks was not such a long time, after all, and with Christmas in between it would soon pass. Reaching for her handbag she repaired her damaged make-up and when Brad entered later in the morning was able to face him calmly.

At lunchtime Helen and Philip were already in the dining-room. 'What happened this morning?' said Helen immediately. 'We could hear your voices. It was all I could do to stop Philip coming in and setting about Brad.'

'It was nothing,' answered Laura with deliberate casualness. 'I wanted to leave, but Brad won't let me— not until my contract's up.'

'I shouldn't think so, either,' Helen was indignant, 'not with Christmas next week. Philip's going back to London today, but he's returning for the holidays. It should be fun.'

'Why do you want to go, anyway?' mocked Philip. 'You're not giving up?'

'There's not much else I can do,' retorted Laura wryly. 'You don't know how upsetting it is working so close to him. It's even worse now he knows you're engaged to Helen.'

'How's that?' asked Helen. 'I thought it might help, and that he'd immediately pop the question before some other young man came along and snapped you up.'

Laura laughed. 'You must be joking. He feels sorry for me, that's all—and his pity is worse than all his harsh words.'

'Poor Laura, I wish we could help. It must be hell

loving a person who doesn't return your love. I'm glad you love me, Philip.' She leaned across the table and kissed him. Laura, watching, thought how marvellous it would be if such a relationship existed between her and Brad, then scolded herself for allowing these thoughts to enter her mind. At one time, before her meeting with Philip, it had seemed faintly possible, but fate had decreed otherwise and this she must learn to accept.

The following days were the most unbearable that Laura had so far experienced. Brad was kindness itself. He made sure she did not overwork, apologising for any errors she made, insisting it must have been his own fault, and spending a few hours each evening in her company, relating anecdotes or amusing experiences—anything to try and cheer her up. But she knew his good will was born of compassion, and this she did not want. She tried hard not to let him see how his consideration affected her, noticing on one or two occasions how her coolness hurt him. But she took refuge in maintaining an outwardly indifferent attitude. It was the only way she could hide her feelings.

On Friday Helen went out and returned with a giant Christmas tree. 'It doesn't look as though Brad's going to bother this year—let's see what we can do to brighten the place up. I'm sure there's a box of trimmings in the attic.'

They spent all evening decorating the tree and fastening up the decorations. A joyful, happy evening when Laura was able to forget her problems for a few hours, until Helen said :

'I can't understand Brad.' She was balancing precariously on the step-ladders trying to fasten an enormous star on top of the tree. 'He's usually the first to suggest dressing up the old house, except last year, of course. With me in bed, no one bothered.'

'Perhaps he's too busy?' ventured Laura. 'How about this holly here?'

'What—oh, fine. Of course he's not busy! He's always found time before. I guess he still disapproves of my engagement. I've noticed how considerate he is towards you, though. Are things improving?',

Laura paused, sucking her finger where a holly leaf had drawn blood. 'It depends how you look at it. On the surface we're good friends, and he certainly doesn't shout at me these days, but it's only because he's sorry for me—and you know how I feel about that.'

'Yes. It's quite a problem. Why don't you let him see how you feel? Who knows, he may be in love with you but afraid to admit it.'

'And pigs will fly,' scoffed Laura. 'No, thank you. He'd probably laugh at me and say *Not another foolish female.*'

'I don't know so much,' said Helen, climbing down and preparing to put the steps away. 'I just think he needs a jog in the right direction. Perhaps if I had a word with—'

'Oh no, you don't,' said Laura in horror, 'I shall be gone in a week, and then I'll be able to forget all about Brad.'

Who she was trying to convince Laura did not know. For the rest of her life there would be only one person who mattered. She would undoubtedly meet other men, might even some day marry one of them, but a part of her heart would always belong to Brad.

Philip returned on Christmas Eve and over dinner Laura was aware of Brad watching her reaction to his presence. Such close scrutiny caused her heartbeats to quicken and she talked more than usual to try and hide her confusion. But apparently this only served to confirm Brad's suspicions that she still cared for Philip, for he squeezed her hand sympathetically, whispering, 'Try not to let him upset you, my dear. I know it's hard, but you mustn't let him spoil your enjoyment.'

At Brad's touch Laura's hand quivered. She tried to pull away, but he held her more tightly. 'I'm all right,' she said unsteadily. 'I appreciate your concern, but honestly there's no need for it. I'm quite capable of managing my own affairs.'

He raised a disbelieving eyebrow. 'You are?' He released her hand, but she noticed he continued to watch her closely for the rest of the evening.

Christmas Day dawned bright and clear. The sun shone and the whole house glittered and sparkled as if it too wanted to join in the festivities.

Laura dressed carefully in her new green mohair sweater and darker green skirt. She brushed her hair until it swung like a silken curtain about her shoulders, and after much deliberation decided to leave it loose. Since the evening when Philip had drawn attention to her hair she had been careful to keep it fastened neatly back, but now, what did it matter? A sudden recklessness took hold of her; she knew how attractive it looked framing her face. 'Let's see what you make of this, Brad Stuart,' she said to herself as she went downstairs.

The other three were already in the dining-room and cries of *Merry Christmas* greeted her. Philip kissed her warmly on the cheek, it was Brad to whom she looked. His smile was friendly and she noticed his eyes flicker over her hair, but he made no attempt to touch her. He wore a black polo-necked sweater and light grey slacks, and her pulses quickened at the sight of him. His muscles rippled beneath the close-fitting jumper and again she marvelled at his physical fitness.

It was not until after breakfast that gifts were exchanged. Helen was delighted with the bag and in return gave Laura a silk scarf. Philip gave her a bottle of perfume, expressing great satisfaction in her choice of cuff-links, and Mrs. Jennings was so overcome with her present that she cried. 'I didn't expect anything,' she said, and it was some minutes before she was her usual self again.

Laura had to confess that she was a little disappointed when she received no present from Brad—although she had not really expected one, and was thankful that she had not bought him anything. It made things easier all round.

After the excitement had died down and Helen and Philip were talking together near the window, Brad drew Laura to one side, pressing a carefully wrapped packet into her hand. She looked up, astonished. Brad had bought her a present after all! Could it be that—? No. He was merely being kind because of her broken engagement. He hoped to cheer her up, make her forget her supposedly broken heart.

With fingers that trembled she slipped off the satin ribbon and opened the shiny paper. Lifting the lid of the tiny box, Laura looked at the exquisite gold and jade pendant. It was lovely, but she couldn't accept it. She knew it was valuable and wondered again at Brad's decision to give it to her.

'It's beautiful,' she breathed, 'but I can't keep it. It's far too—too—'

'Too what?' he cut in softly. 'It belonged to my mother. She had auburn hair just like your own. It will suit you as well as it suited her, especially against that green jumper. As soon as I saw you in it I knew the pendant was exactly right. No—I insist you keep it—as a token of my thanks for the good work you've put in. Here, let me put it on for you.'

With gentle fingers he lifted her hair and slipped the gold chain into place. Laura quivered at his touch. It was as though every nerve end was on fire and she struggled against the desire to press her body against his. To feel his virile strength and steady beating of his heart against her own. Her lips trembled as she smiled her thanks. 'It's very kind of you, Brad, but are you sure it shouldn't belong to Helen? Wouldn't your mother have wished that?'

'If she'd met you, she would have desired you to have it, I know. Please believe me,' he pleaded.

It took every ounce of Laura's self-control to maintain an outward calm, not to let him see the love in her eyes. But she wished the reason for his giving her the pendant had been different. She didn't want thanks. He paid her to work for him. Those few carelessly spoken words dimmed her initial happiness; spoilt what would have been a cherished memory in the years to come.

She moved away to where Helen stood watching, a peculiar expression in her grey eyes.

'You don't mind?' Laura's voice held concern. Her hand touched the pendant—she knew she should not have accepted it.

For a second Helen seemed puzzled, and then realised that Laura referred to the necklace. 'Oh, that! Of course not. You'll appreciate it far more than me. I like modern jewellery.'

'Then why were you looking at me so strangely?' asked Laura, sensing something different about Brad's sister.

Helen suddenly laughed. 'You'll find out, soon. It's very true that love is blind.'

'I don't know what you're talking about,' said Laura huffily. Looking at Philip she noticed that he too was smiling, a secret smile. What was the matter with them both? she thought crossly. What was going on? 'I'm going up to my room,' she said stiffly. 'My arm's bothering me this morning. I'll see you at lunch.'

Brad had his back to her as she left. 'I don't suppose he's even noticed that I've gone,' she grumbled as she climbed the stairs. 'Why did I ever agree to stay on? I should have stuck to my decision and left.'

In her room she studied her reflection in the dressing-table mirror: green eyes looked pensively back. She touched the necklace, as if by so doing she could bring Brad nearer. Her vision misted as tears gathered and for a while she allowed them to fall. Time and time again her heart called out, 'Why, oh, why did I have to fall in love with you?'

She did not realise that she had spoken the words out loud. Nor did she hear the door gently open and soft footsteps cross the carpet. She jumped violently as a hand touched her shoulder. 'Don't cry. I can't bear to see you upset.'

Laura's heart seemed to stop beating. She dabbed ineffectively at her tears with her knuckles. A large handkerchief was pressed into her hands. Carefully she wiped her wet face, before raising swollen eyes to counter Brad's penetrating gaze through the mirror.

What on earth was he doing here? She felt suddenly breathless. Why had he followed her? She was unable to turn away from the magnetism of his eyes, and felt as though she were watching a scene from a play as he caught her shoulders and turned her round to face him, dropping to his knees beside her.

'Laura, my love. Forget him. You'd never have been happy.'

Her lips trembled as she saw the concern on his face, and her carefully built defences crumbled. With one swift movement he gathered her into his arms. 'Oh, Brad,' she cried as his lips sought hers. He kissed her and it was as though time stood still. As though no one else existed in the whole universe.

Afterwards they drew apart and Brad spoke softly, as if afraid to spoil the magic of the moment. 'Let me take care of you, Laura. Let me teach you to forget Philip.'

Her heartbeats quickened. 'I don't know what you mean.'

'I'm asking you to marry me, silly,' he said, running a finger gently down her cheek.

'B-but you don't love me.' Her voice was a mere whisper.

'That's where you're wrong. I do love you. I've loved you ever since the day you arrived—mud-stained, cross and tired.'

Laura looked at him in wonder. Had she heard correctly? Was the culmination of all her dreams about to come true? 'I don't believe it,' she breathed. 'Y-you love *me*?'

'Very much, my sweet Laura. I wanted to tell you then, but decided to wait—to try and win your love. I was vain enough to think I was succeeding until the day I came to the flat and found you with Philip. I felt like kicking him in the teeth.'

'But I explained that,' said Laura anxiously. 'In fact I never wanted him there at all, and as soon as you'd gone I turned him out.'

Brad raised his eyebrows. 'I wish I'd known, but I'm afraid I didn't believe you. It looked such an intimate little scene I couldn't believe it was the first time he'd been there. And when you went off with him in the restaurant I decided there was no chance for me at all.'

'I'm sorry,' she whispered, 'but you annoyed me, and I did it more out of spite than anything else.'

He shook his head sadly, as if bewildered by the whole affair, moving to go and sit on the bed. 'I spent a miserable week at home trying to get you out of my mind, and in the end I decided to take a trip to Africa. New faces, new surroundings. Even then I rang you at the last minute to see if you'd say anything to make me change my mind. Remember? You left me in little doubt as to how you felt.' He stared down at his hands. 'It didn't work, Africa. You were like a drug to my mind. I wanted you desperately and came back determined to ask you to marry me—only to find that you had become engaged to Philip during my absence.'

Brad's hurt was mirrored in his eyes and Laura strove hard to stop herself from hurtling across the few feet of carpet into his arms, declaring that she too loved him. There was so much that was not yet clear, and Brad obviously wanted to make a clean breast of everything.

'I think I knew, even then, that there was something wrong,' he continued, 'for I couldn't let you leave. I used your contract to keep you in the hope that something would happen to make you turn to me.'

'Poor Brad,' she said softly, but he appeared not to notice her interruption.

'Gradually I realised I was right. You didn't look or act like a woman in love, and when Philip paid attention to Helen you didn't mind. I tried to find out why, but you'd erected a prickly fence round yourself and I couldn't get near.'

'Brad,' Laura's voice quivered, 'I'd no idea how you felt. If only you'd given me some intimation.'

'How could I, when we were always arguing? Anyway I knew you had no feelings for me, I proved that the day Helen returned home. I was convinced I could make you respond. It hurt terribly when you didn't.'

'I'm sorry. I wanted you to kiss me—but—'

'I know. You're a very loyal person and I hated him for the way he was treating you. When Helen rang from London to say she was staying for the week I went down to find out for myself exactly what was going on.'

'She never said,' gasped Laura.

'She didn't know,' grimly.

'You—you mean you spied on them?' Astonished that he could behave in such an underhand manner, Laura stared, wide-eyed.

'Precisely. But even though I had proof I still couldn't bring myself to tell you. I spent hours trying to think of the best way to save your pride. Then when they returned the matter was taken out of my hands—and you admitted you knew. Was that why you were so miserable?'

'N-not really,' confessed Laura. 'I-I'd got other things on my mind.' Everything had become startlingly clear. All the time Brad had loved her! His bad tempers, his sharp words, had all been a result of jealousy. If only her hasty temper had not led her into a fictitious engagement, there would have been no need for the heartache she had suffered. She could have been sheltered in the warmth of his love—might even now have been his wife. She shivered deliciously at the thought, but all was not yet over. So far he had not given her much chance to speak, but she would have to confess to her deception before she felt free to accept the love he was offering.

'I'm not an ogre, Laura.' He spoke pleadingly. 'I know you don't love me—but given time I'm sure you'll learn.'

She could see the love in his eyes. The pain in her heart was almost unbearable. She crossed to his side and gently touched his face. 'I've no need to learn, Brad, my darling. I—I love you already.'

He caught her roughly to him. 'By all the gods, I can't believe it.' Then just as suddenly he pushed her away. 'But I don't understand. Surely you're not so fickle that you can fall in and out of love at the drop of a hat?'

Laura bit her lip anxiously. 'I'm sorry, Brad, I deceived you. Philip and I were never in love.'

'But you were going to marry him?'

'No—I told you he had asked me—which was perfectly true. You assumed the rest, and like a fool I let you go on believing it.'

'What made you say it in the first place?' Brad frowned.

'A desire to hurt you when you thought I was crying over Philip.'

'You certainly did that. My world was shattered.' He still looked puzzled. 'Then why were you crying?'

Laura smiled weakly. 'I was crying for a love I thought I'd never know. I was crying for you, my darling. I'd loved you so long—ever since the night you scolded me for getting my feet wet. Yes—' as he raised surprised eyebrows. 'But I thought you hated me. I thought you'd laugh if you found out I'd joined the ranks—so I was determined to hide my feelings.'

'Which you did admirably. If only I'd known.' He rose, pulling her close. 'I shudder when I think how very nearly I let you go. I hated to play the part of the hard-hearted boss, but I was determined to make one last effort to win your love.' His hands slid round her back and with a moan Laura cradled her head against his chest.

'What fools we've been,' he breathed hoarsely, 'how much time we've wasted. There's still so much I don't understand, but at the moment I don't care.'

She raised her lips to his, and a deep silence filled the room as in their united love they found true happiness.

romance is beautiful!

and Harlequin Reader Service is your passport to the Heart of Harlequin

Harlequin is the world's leading publisher of romantic fiction novels. If you enjoy the mystery and adventure of romance, then you will want to keep up to date on all of our new monthly releases—eight brand new Romances and four Harlequin Presents.

If you are interested in catching up on exciting and valuable back issues, Harlequin Reader Service offers a wide choice of best-selling novels reissued for your reading enjoyment.

If you want a truly jumbo read and a money-saving value, the Harlequin Omnibus offers three intriguing novels under one cover by one of your favorite authors.

To find out more about Harlequin, the following information will be your passport to the Heart of Harlequin.

the omnibus

A Great Idea! Three great romances by the same author, in one deluxe paperback volume.

A Great Value! Almost 600 pages of pure entertainment for only $1.95 per volume.

Essie Summers

Bride in Flight (#933)
...begins on the eve of Kirsty's wedding with the strange phone call that changed her life. Blindly, instinctively Kirsty ran — but even New Zealand wasn't far enough to avoid the complications that followed!

Postscript to Yesterday (#1119)
...Nicola was dirty, exasperated and a little bit frightened. She was in no shape after her amateur mechanics on the car to meet any man, let alone Forbes Westerfield. He was the man who had told her not to come.

Meet on My Ground (#1326)
...is the story of two people in love, separated by pride. Alastair Campbell had money and position — Sarah Macdonald was a girl with pride. But pride was no comfort to her at all after she'd let Alastair go!

Jean S. MacLeod

The Wolf of Heimra (#990)
...Fenella knew that in spite of her love for the island, she had no claim on Heimra yet — until an heir was born. These MacKails were so sure of themselves; they expected everything to come their way.

Summer Island (#1314)
...Cathie's return to Loch Arden was traumatic. She knew she was clinging to the past, refusing to let it go. But change was something you thought of happening in other places — never in your own beloved glen.

Slave of the Wind (#1339)
...Lesley's pleasure on homecoming and meeting the handsome stranger quickly changed to dismay when she discovered that he was Maxwell Croy — the man whose family once owned her home. And Maxwell was determined to get it back again.

Susan Barrie

Marry a Stranger (#1034)
...if she lived to be a hundred, Stacey knew she'd never be more violently in love than she was at this moment. But Edouard had told her bluntly that he would never fall in love with her!

Rose in the Bud (#1168)
...One thing Cathleen learned in Venice: it was highly important to be cautious when a man was a stranger and inhabited a world unfamiliar to her. The more charm he possessed, the more wary she should be!

The Marriage Wheel (#1311)
...Admittedly the job was unusual — lady chauffeur to Humphrey Lestrode; and admittedly Humphrey was high-handed and arrogant. Nevertheless Frederica was enjoying her work at Farthing Hall. Then along came her mother and beautiful sister, Rosaleen, to upset everything.

Violet Winspear

Beloved Tyrant (#1032)
...Monterey was a beautiful place to recuperate. Lyn's job was interesting. Everything, in fact, would have been perfect, Lyn Gilmore thought, if it hadn't been for the hateful Rick Corderas. He made her feel alive again!

Court of the Veils (#1267)
...In the lush plantation on the edge of the Sahara, Roslyn Brant tried very hard to remember her fiancé and her past. But the bitter, disillusioned Duane Hunter refused to believe that she ever was engaged to his cousin, Armand.

Palace of the Peacocks (#1318)
...Suddenly the island, this exotic place that so recently had given her sanctuary, seemed an unlucky place rather than a magical one. She must get away from the cold palace and its ghost — and especially from Ryk van Helden.

Isobel Chace

The Saffron Sky (#1250)
...set in a tiny village skirting the exotic Bangkok, Siam, the small, nervous Myfanwy Jones realizes her most cherished dream, adventure and romance in a far-off land. Two handsome men determine to marry her, but both have the same mysterious reason....

A Handful of Silver (#1306)
...in exciting Rio de Janeiro, city of endless beaches and skyscraper hotels, a battle of wits is waged between Madelaine Delahaye, Pilar Fernandez, the jealous fiancée of her childhood friend, and her handsome, treacherous cousin — Luis da Maestro....

The Damask Rose (#1334)
...Vicki Tremaine flies to the heady atmosphere of Damascus to meet Adam Templeton, fiancé of the rebellious Miriam. But alas, as time passes, Vicki only becomes more attracted to this young Englishman with the steel-like personality....

information please

**All the Exciting News from
Under the Harlequin Sun**

It costs you nothing to receive our news bulletins and intriguing brochures. From our brand new releases to our money-saving 3-in-1 omnibus and valuable best-selling back titles, our information package is sure to be a hit. Don't miss out on any of the exciting details. Send for your Harlequin INFORMATION PLEASE package today.